The forest was dark and foreboding, and the huge old trees with gnarled limbs and spiky branches stood like sentries, guarding its entrance.

Jessie strained her eyes to see more clearly. It was so dark. But suddenly, lightning struck. Thunder roared as streaks of silver flashed across the sky. The rain fell in torrents that slammed against the earth. It was then at the height of the storm that Jessie saw her beloved horse, Time-Out, suddenly starting to run in a state of terror.

"Noooo," Jessie screamed, trying in vain to break through so that Time-Out could hear her. But Time-Out just kept running along the slippery path toward the wide ravine, where it was impossible to see what, if anything, was on the other side.

"Help!" Jessie leaped up in bed, truly frightened. Little beads of sweat laced her forehead, and her entire body was shaking. Jessie looked over at her friend Lynne who was sleeping peacefully. Reaching up to wipe a tear from the corner of her eye, she couldn't believe how real the nightmare had seemed. And just then, she was shocked to see Lynne's mother, barefoot and in her nightgown, beckoning her downstairs.

"You've got a telephone call, Jessie. It's your friend, Kate," she called.

"Oh no," Jessie wailed, and flew down the stairs. She was convinced that something was the matter with Time-Out. . . .

Other Fawcett Girls Only Titles:

BLUE RIBBON #5
TIME-OUT FOR JESSIE

Chris St. John

FAWCETT GIRLS ONLY • NEW YORK

RLI: $\dfrac{\text{VL: 5 \& up}}{\text{IL: 5 \& up}}$

A Fawcett Girls Only Book
Published by Ballantine Books
Copyright © 1989 by Cloverdale Press, Inc.

Library of Congress Catalog Card Number: 89-91166

ISBN 0-449-13456-3

Manufactured in the United States of America

First Edition: August 1989

 **Chapter 1**

JESSIE ROBESON and her deep brown bay, Time-Out, stood perfectly still in a corner of the practice ring at Windcroft Stables and watched Dara Cooper and her horse, Arpeggio, go through their final dressage test once again. Jessie and her two friends, Dara and Kate Wiley, had finished their usual afternoon lesson with trainer Anne Wiley, who also happened to be Kate's mother. Today they had put in an extra hour and a half of dressage practice in preparation for next weekend's combined training competition.

Dara and Arpeggio looked very smooth as they moved from a trot to a canter, and then performed a near-perfect shoulder-in that was square, relaxed, and attentive.

"Great!" Kate shouted. "Looks good. But you've still got to work on your circles." Kate was acting as observer and critic for both Jessie and Dara. It was something they all took turns doing, and in the process they had developed respect for one another's opinions. In fact, just this year Jessie began to realize how much she relied on her two friends, and how lucky she was to have them.

"It's your turn," Kate said, and Jessie and Time-Out stepped into the ring. "Try another halt. Last time you used too much inside rein. The judges won't miss that on Saturday."

"Come on, Time-Out, let's get it right this time," Jessie whispered to her horse as they stepped into position for the lateral movement. She, for one, was exhausted, but still determined to keep trying until they did it right.

And it was worth the effort. This time they rode a neat corner and moved into a circle before executing a halt that was absolutely precise. "Well done," both Kate and Dara applauded.

"Do that again on Saturday and you aren't going to stay Novice for long," Kate reassured her.

Jessie grinned broadly, and Time-Out whinnied her response to their approval. If Jessie was proud of anything it was that after Time-Out's colt was weaned and they had resumed conditioning, her movements—and halts—had been brought back to near-perfection within an impossibly short time.

"I swear, that horse must have been doing some heavy mental training during her pregnancy," Dara remarked from where she now sat perched on the rail fence that circled the ring. "She looks even better than she did before she had Chesapeake."

"It's the same with horses as it is with people," Kate said knowingly. "Some of them thrive on motherhood."

"Yeah. Well, once was enough for this kid,"

Jessie laughed as she slipped down off Time-Out's back. "After all, we've got a full-time career in eventing."

Although it would still be a while before Time-Out completely recovered the muscle tone she had before foaling her colt, her comeback was uncanny, and Jessie was regaining her confidence.

"Mom says we can use the three-horse van when we go to Massachusetts next weekend," Kate said as both she and Dara followed Jessie and Time-Out into the barn. They had cooled down Spy and Arpeggio already, and now were just hanging around waiting for Jessie to stable her horse.

"That's great," Jessie sighed deeply, hoping that her relief wasn't too apparent. It had been hard enough convincing her father to let her accompany Kate and Dara to the competition in Ogden, Massachusetts, a four-hour trip each way. It would mean missing a day of school and a weekend of chores, but Mr. Robeson had agreed as long as the expenses were minimal. The use of the Windcroft trailer meant that Jessie probably wouldn't have to worry about the cost of transporting Time-Out. One more problem solved. Also—thanks to Anne—they were all invited to stay in the home of a friend of hers, so the question of lodging was settled.

"Are you and Spy ready to take another beating?" Dara asked Kate as she swung back and forth from a cross beam atop an empty stall.

"More than ready, thank you," Kate snapped back. She and Dara were always competing neck and neck at the horse trials, and bantering about it was an ongoing activity. "Everyone knows that Spy and I could have taken this entire month off, even gone down to Florida to soak up some sun, and could still whip you and Arpeggio blindfolded." She turned up her nose haughtily, but couldn't suppress a laugh.

"If I remember correctly," Dara retaliated, "the blue ribbon from the last competition was presented to me and Arpeggio. I vaguely remember you and Night Owl coming in a mere second."

"By a hair, by a hair," Kate retorted, gesturing with her thumb against forefinger to remind Dara that, in fact, they had beaten her by two points. Kate realized that Dara's abilities presented her with a challenge to work hard, and that theirs was a truly positive form of competition. She didn't really care how many ribbons she won; her goal was to get to the Olympics someday, and Dara's inadvertent nipping at her heels was helping her get there.

"This time's going to be different, though," Jessie reminded them as she brushed Time-Out's coat to a gleaming shine. She felt like an artist, polishing Time-Out's deep brown coat to a beautiful gleam that brought out the graceful lines of her conformation, and her horse loved the pampering. "This time," Jessie repeated, "Kate's going to be riding the unbeatable Northern Spy."

"Big deal," said Dara, a little too confidently.

Everyone remembered how Jessie had bagged a blue ribbon in a recent competition riding Spy in a Novice Division. Jessie had been very reluctant to ride him because he was so independent and powerful. And after it was over, it seemed as if he had won the contest all by himself, as if she had been a mere accomplice to a born winner. Spy had given the audience a breathless dressage performance and a no-fault in either jumping phase.

"Yeah. It looks like my days on Night Owl have come to an end," Kate interjected in a more serious note. Jessie and Dara knew how much she loved Night Owl, and how bad Kate felt at the prospect of having to leave him behind. It had taken her a long time to accept the fact that she could never get to the Olympics on that horse, even though he had come a long way. Good fortune had brought Spy on the scene just when Kate needed him.

"Here you are, baby, a nice clean stall," Jessie cooed to Time-Out as she finally decided she had been curried and brushed to perfection. "Got some nice, fresh water for you, too," she said as she closed the door and reached up to give her a good-bye pat on the forehead.

"Yuck," Dara said, completing her acrobatics on the beam with an attempt to leap clear across the barn. "The way you talk to that horse, it's a wonder she's not a total wimp ... like some guys I know." She gave Jessie a playful poke in the ribs as they stomped out into the late afternoon light.

"Oh, no. You aren't going to bring *that* up again, I hope," Jessie moaned. The three friends sauntered together toward the steps of the Wileys' back porch.

"It's good for you to talk about it," Dara insisted as she bent down to tie her shoe. "After all, losing Amory isn't the end of the world, and you're

going to have to see him someday. Like today,
maybe?"

"I think she's about to have an ice-cream at-
tack," Kate predicted with a giggle. "It's been
twenty-four hours since her last cone. That darn
Amory *would* have to work at Lickety-Split," she
sighed, and offered Jessie a sympathetic glance.

"Come on, we're going in to wash up," Dara
said.

"I'll be right there," Jessie said as she leaned
against the step and stretched out her long legs.
She needed a few minutes alone. The late afternoon view of the Wiley's back acreage and stables was spectacular; like a photo from a Sierra
Club calendar, she thought. In the foreground, tall
poplars that had been planted as windbreakers
stood straight and regal, and in the distance the
dark silhouettes of grazing horses cut the golden
sky into flat, irregular shapes.

Jessie searched her heart and knew she wasn't
really unhappy about Amory, but she had to sort
out just what had happened between them. Sure,
she had been interested in him, Jessie had to
admit to herself. For one thing, he was cute, and
he was also enthusiastic about her riding. Hadn't
he been terribly excited when she'd showed her
classmates the blue ribbons she'd won on Spy?
Jessie remembered the day when Amory had finally asked her out. They had decided to double-
date with Pete and Kate, who had been stuck on
each other forever, it seemed.

Not being used to going out because, after all,
she had just started dating, Jessie also remembered how nervous she'd been when she opened

the door and saw Amory standing there, looking no less than terrified himself. Her father had been anything but diplomatic, and Jessie almost died when he made Amory sit down to be quizzed about everything except his private birthmarks for over half an hour.

When they finally left, things should have gotten better, and Jessie had thought the worst was over. But even though she'd been excited about going to a movie and then out for pizza, the whole date suddenly went flat. She and Amory simply didn't hit it off. And it didn't help much to have Kate and Pete mooning over each other like two lovesick calves. In contrast to the sparks that were flying between Kate and Pete, Jessie felt as if Amory could have been her brother. When the evening had finally ended and Amory had dropped her off, Jessie had been relieved it was over.

Dara couldn't believe the night had bombed so badly. "Sure, I spend a lot of time with Arpeggio, too," Dara had exclaimed with impatience when, instead of a tale of romance and intrigue, she had received a bland review of a bum date. "But I'm not totally hung up on my horse like you are. I bet that all the time you were out with Amory you were thinking about Time-Out, or about the competition."

"On the other hand," Kate had said, realizing that Jessie really did feel bad, "who cares about that boring Amory. He'll wind up scooping ice cream all his life, if he doesn't wise up."

Deep down, Jessie hadn't really cared. It was true: Time-Out did require all of her attention now, and if she was ever going to move from

Novice to the Training level, she had to concentrate all her efforts on putting in as much time as possible in the practice ring.

"The worst thing about Ogden will be the cross-country." Jessie's thoughts were suddenly interrupted by Kate's remark as she and Dara came back out on the porch. "Hey, what have you been daydreaming about, Jes?" Kate asked.

"Oh, just thinking about all those ditches and drop fences at Ogden," Jessie fibbed.

"Sure. I'll buy that," Kate teased. "Now let's talk business. It's a long course and I'd like to try and walk it more than once before the meet," she said.

"When are you going to do that? In the middle of the night?" Dara piped in. "Anyway, we know Spy could ford the Mississippi or jump the Grand Canyon with no practice at all."

"Oh, no. Not again!" Jessie rolled her eyes. They were back to where the conversation had begun, to where all their conversations seemed to begin and end. On the subject of horses and competitions. The three girls exchanged glances and then began to laugh.

"Well, I can't stand it another minute," Dara almost screamed as she leapt up from the porch. "After a workout like this one, I need ice cream!"

"Me, too," Kate agreed as she stood up and dusted off the front of her jeans. "If we leave right away, we can get to Lickety-Split just in time to ruin our appetite for dinner."

"Yeah, and when Anne asks, it was your idea," Dara pointed a finger at Jessie. "Okay?"

"Forget it," Jessie said. "You two go on ahead. I

have to get home and make dinner. I don't have the time to go gallivanting around, constantly eating ice cream. Besides,"—she shook out her shoulder-length mane—"I don't intend to have any trouble getting into my jodhpurs next weekend."

Kate and Dara ran toward Dara's car as Jessie walked toward the stable to retrieve her bicycle and start off for home. She felt very tired, realizing she really did have to cook dinner, do some laundry, *and* hit the books. If she could also clean the den tonight, she would have clear sailing for the weekend. With the housekeeper gone, it seemed as if there were no limits to the work Jessie had been delegated to do.

"I guess if we do well this weekend, it'll help," Jessie confided in Time-Out before leaving. As usual, the horse stuck out her neck and dangled her head over Jessie's back in her own type of horse hug. "If we bring home another blue, that should make Dad happy," she said wistfully. But the expression on Jessie's face was far from confident as she realized the enormousness of her responsibility as a virtual replacement for her mother at home, an honor student, and a committed championship rider. "There's not enough time ..." she whispered to her horse, patting her on the nose. Then, as an antidote to her despair, she added, "But I've got you now, Time-Out. I've got a horse of my own. And no problem is too big for us to handle—as long as we tackle it together ..."

Chapter 2

"TIME-OUT! Be still!" Jessie commanded firmly as she gave her horse her final hosing down. "I thought you liked baths."

Jessie looked down at the pair of overalls she wore over her clothes when she cleaned stalls or washed Time-Out. The front of her pants was sopping wet. "I got more water on me than I did on you!" She laughed, and gave Time-Out's rump a friendly pat.

"Looking good," Kate declared as she approached the stables. "She's all done now, isn't she? I saw you washing her tail and mane on Tuesday, so it wouldn't be too slippery to braid."

It was now Thursday afternoon, and Jessie felt as if she had been working continuously, night and day, to get everything ready for the show. "All I have to do tomorrow morning is make sure her tack is spic-and-span," Jessie said.

"Gee," Kate replied. "Time-Out really does look gorgeous. I hope I can get Spy looking this nifty."

Jessie eyed Kate suspiciously. "Hey," she asked, "why are you laying it on so thick? Sounds like you might want something.

"Out with it, Kate. What is it?" Jessie demanded, when Kate didn't answer.

"Well," Kate said, kicking the dirt, "I was wondering if you could help me with my braids. I know you have a lot to do, but I can never get Spy's tail quite right." She paused. "Like you can."

"Oh, man," Jessie moaned. "Do me a favor and don't try that buttering-up routine on anyone else. It won't work." Then she added quickly, "All right. But if I do it, don't forget you'll owe me one."

"Absolutely no problem," Kate declared. "Your jacket's in the cleaners, isn't it? I'm going into town to pick up mine, and I'll get yours, too. How's that for a trade-off?"

"Wow. I almost forgot, I was so busy getting my horse ready to go, I forgot about myself. Thanks, Kate. I've got to get home right away and wash my jodhpurs and shirt so they'll dry by tomorrow."

"Calm down, Jessie. We're gonna make it. We always do. If I don't see you again tonight, be here early in the morning. We gotta be on the road by noon to get to Ogden in time to walk the cross-country course. I guess you'll wait till morning to wrap Time-Out's legs for the trip?"

"Yeah. She won't want to stay bandaged all night. Your mom was nice enough to loan me a tail guard, so that takes care of that problem." And Jessie had saved enough money to buy a sheet for the trip so Time-Out would stay clean.

"Great. Oh, Jessie, I can't wait!" Kate exclaimed

suddenly. She could barely keep from jumping up and down with excitement.

Jessie couldn't agree more. There was nothing more fun than getting ready for a competition. But it could also really rattle the nerves, and right now Jessie felt like an overinflated balloon, just about to pop!

Somehow she managed to finish with Time-Out and get home in time to wash her own clothing and pack. Jessie's younger sister, Sarah, helped with the packing and was just as excited as Jessie. "Jessie," Sara asked sleepily, when Jessie finally tucked her in to bed that evening, "If you win another ribbon, could I bring it to school again?"

"Sure thing," Jessie replied, hugging her sister. "One of these days I'll even take you with me to a show," she promised before she turned out the light.

Unfortunately, her father's support wasn't as wholehearted as Sarah's. His unusually stony silence during dinner told Jessie he had a lot on his mind, including plans for how he was going to take care of housework and cooking during the three days she was not going to be there. Their housekeeper had quit, and that left only Jessie and her father to oversee both house and family. Jessie was going to bring it up at dinner, but then she decided that she would wait until her father said something, and in the meantime, try not to feel guilty. After all, she had her own life to lead and a competition to win. If she got upset now, she could easily mess up her concentration, and even throw the show.

* * *

"All right, the van is ready. You can lead her up the ramp now," Anne said to Jessie.

"Come on, girl," Jessie cooed as she urged Time-Out into the van. Jessie was always a little nervous when traveling with her horse, and could understand Time-Out's claustrophobia from having to stand still in such a small space for four hours of traveling.

Time-Out snorted her response as she entered the van, and Jessie quieted her as best she could.

It seemed like only moments later when they were on their way. Jessie finally relaxed as she looked out the window at the pretty landscape. It wasn't long before she conked out to the familiar sound of Dara and Kate's carrying on about who was going to come home with what ribbon. When she woke up, they were already in Massachusetts.

Jessie wasn't really fully awake when they reached Ogden, a pretty town nestled among rolling green hills. The first priority the moment they got there was, of course, to see how the horses were doing. There was a front window in the van, so the girls had been able to keep an eye on them during the trip, but the moment the ramp was let down it was obvious they had had enough, and Time-Out, Arpeggio, and Spy all stomped and snorted their preferences to be the first one out.

Luckily there was enough time to exercise the horses before the girls checked in, got their dressage numbers and cross-country pinnies, and began to walk the course. Time-Out did seem tired from the ride, and Jessie was anxious to get her settled in her stall and groomed for the evening so they all could rest. She would have to do Spy's braiding before dinner, and after that, it was a matter of relying on all their hard work and, of course, good old Lady Luck.

She took a minute to gobble down a sandwich and apple and then heard Kate announce that they were about to begin walking the course. Jessie was confident that, between the three of them, they would catch any uneven terrain, holes, or tricky turns. Part of the course was heavily wooded, and another stretch was over open field, so they were also going to have to pay particular attention to a few dark corners and sudden changes in light. Jessie knew that Kate, in particular, had no worries because cross-country was Spy's strongest area. Dara, on the other hand, had to be sharp. Arpeggio was best in dressage, and maintaining an even pace through the cross-country course could be his biggest challenge, especially after his fall.

Later that evening, when they were finally settled in for the night at the home of Anne's friends, the Dobkinses, they talked about possible problems they might encounter.

"Don't forget to take the first jump on the right because of the slope on the left-hand side of the path," Kate said as she donned her flowered pajamas. "The other fences are straight forward and clear sailing, as far as I could see, but the course is anything but flat," she concluded with a somewhat tired sigh.

"Oh, we're all going to be just great," Jessie said confidently. She sat on the bed brushing her shiny brown hair.

"Oh, Jessie," Dara joined in. "You're such an optimist. You can't possibly be as cool and contained as you're pretending to be the night before a competition."

"Hey, what's the point of getting hysterical? There's nothing more we can do now. Either we're ready, or we're not."

"Well, how do you do, Ms. Poise of the Year," Dara teased. Jessie smiled and curtsied, and then grabbed a pillow off the bed and sent it flying all the way across the room at Dara.

The pillow fight was under way, and Jessie, Kate, and Dara were laughing and screaming at the top of their lungs! It was Kate who realized they were making enough noise to wake the dead, much less the other people in the household.

"Shhh," she hissed, and then collapsed into another fit of giggles.

"Ah ... I feel better," Dara said, flopping down on the bed.

"I needed that, too," Jessie agreed. Still, she thought to herself before falling off to sleep, she couldn't remember when she had felt this nervous.

But the next day as she and Time-Out stood waiting in the warm-up ring to be called for cross-country, she couldn't have been calmer. Both horse and rider had woken up to a superb fall Massachusetts day and were feeling magnificent. And their earlier dressage performance had gone very well.

She had braided up Time-Out's mane and tail and finished it with white tape, and she knew that she, too, looked elegant in her white shirt, black coat, and velvet riding hat. Good ol' Anne had

helped her out once again by loaning her a pair
of magnificent riding boots that completed her
outfit to a tee. From the moment they stepped
into the ring, Jessie somehow knew that Time-
Out was up for a good performance. Relaxed on
the bit in dressage, she was both freely forward
and attentive and didn't tense up once. Her impulsion was good and her corners supple, so that
by the time she made her last half turn down the
center line and didn't overshoot it, chances for
any further error were nil. If her halt was square,
they were home free. It was with a great deal of
pride that she saluted the judges, and rode off to
receive the hearty felicitations of her friends.

"That was great!" someone behind her said
when she finally dismounted and stopped to catch
her breath. Jessie turned around to see a familiar-
looking face, a girl who was also competing in
Novice.

"Thanks," Jessie repeated politely. "You're riding Novice, too, aren't you?"

"Yeah," the girl said somewhat flatly. "That's
my chestnut bay over there. Her name's Dolly."

"Wow. She's beautiful!" Jessie exclaimed. "What
a color. Have you done your dressage test yet?"

"Yes, unfortunately. I'm afraid we didn't get off
to a very good start today. We had to strike off
twice after a bad canter, and were behind the bit
till the halt. But, other than that ..."

"Oh, don't feel too bad. I'm sure it was better
than you think. Sorry I missed it."

"Oh, thanks. You're making me feel much better. Maybe we'll make up for it in cross-country.
But I'm afraid Dolly might not be ready for that,
either. She has a tendency to rush her fences."

"Time-Out did that at first, too," Jessie said. "It was only because she was scared. Once she got used to ditches and stone walls—you know the proverbial obstacle course they set up—she was fine."

"By the way, my name's Lynne Stevens. I live here in Ogden. It's nice to meet you." Lynne smiled broadly, obviously feeling better after Jessie's words of encouragement. "It must be time for me to get ready for phase two. I'll look for you later."

"Great," Jessie responded enthusiastically. "And good luck with cross-country."

For the rest of the day, Jessie continued to give ace performances. Time-Out sailed through the cross-country course like Pegasus, with their fastest time ever.

"I think you're ready to move up a notch, kid," Kate remarked after giving her a congratulatory hug. "Time-Out is obviously bored by this Novice routine."

Dara agreed vigorously, and Jessie went back to Time-Out to cool her down and walk off any nervousness. Even though she wasn't blowing hard, she was pretty heated up after all her work, so Jessie decided to give her a quick sponge and brushing before show jumping. She noticed that Lynne, too, had finished the cross-country event and was busy primping Dolly. Jessie stopped to chat with her for a minute.

"I think Dolly and I need more practice." Lynne initiated the conversation as she saw Jessie approaching her.

Jessie smiled understandingly. "How'd you do,

girl?" she addressed Dolly as she ran a hand across her sleek withers. "You've got to be one of the most beautiful chestnuts I've ever seen," she said. "And look at those big brown eyes," she flattered Dolly, who clearly loved all of the attention.

"Well, we rushed a couple of fences again, like I thought, and that high wall on the back side of the course was just too much. She stopped more than three seconds before jumping, so I think I have penalty points."

"Ah, that's okay," Jessie again reassured them. "I know a champ when I see one." And then as an afterthought, "Gee. I'd love to ride her."

"Yikes!" Jessie suddenly exclaimed a moment later. "I've got to get back. We're almost up." She raced over to Time-Out to make sure she was ready for the next event: stadium jumping.

"Let's not get overconfident," Jessie said to both herself and the horse as they stood waiting to be called.

Stadium jumping is a test of obedience, agility, and courage all rolled into one, and Time-Out again came through with flying colors. She jumped calmly and fluently, without pulling at her rider, and it was clear to Jessie in her final salute to the judges that she would be the overall winner. Being a bit superstitious, Jessie decided to wait until the blue ribbon was in her hand before really celebrating. But she knew this was going to be one set of score sheets that were good enough to be framed.

After cooling down Time-Out, Jessie—with her new friend Lynne in tow—watched Kate and Dara compete. In dressage, Arpeggio was not moving freely through his routine. Jessie was surprised that he seemed nervous, and his concentration was slightly off. It must be a result of his accident, she thought.

Jessie saw that Spy, on the other hand, performed the dressage test with amazing suppleness and rhythm. His circles and halts were also near-perfect. While watching the cross-country, Jessie was surprised to see Spy falter. He overextended himself by taking the course too fast, and lost control in the very beginning, so that Kate simply couldn't compensate. She either had to let him go and hope for the best or break to a trot and complete the course slowly—which she did. They wound up having a clear course, but lost points for time.

Kate was disappointed and slightly ticked off at Spy, to say the least. He still thought he was running the show.

"You're just going to have to learn who's boss around here," Kate declared as she walked Spy to cool him down.

As it turned out, Kate still took second, and Dara and Arpeggio won a red ribbon. But the big winner was a handsome guy about their age who was riding a well-trained dappled gray and was obviously ready to move up to the Preliminary level.

"That's Ed York," Lynne told Jessie as they watched him lead his horse out of the ring. "He's my next-door neighbor. His parents own the stables where I board Dolly."

"Oh," Jessie said, unable to hide her interest.

She didn't know who was more fascinating, the rider or the horse, and suddenly realized that somewhere along the line she, like Dara and Kate, was developing a healthy interest in boys.

"I've got an idea," Lynne jumped to her feet. "Why don't you come over to my house for a while. You can see the stables and meet my folks and, you know, just hang out."

"Gee, I'd love to," Jessie responded with enthusiasm. Even though they claimed they weren't hung up on winning, Jessie knew that Kate and Dara would be slightly bummed out by not taking first place in the competition. Besides, it might be fun to expand her friendships, and spend some time with someone else. Maybe she could give Lynne a few pointers, and even get a chance to ride Dolly.

"I'm gonna go call the Dobkinses and make sure it's all right with them," Jessie said excitedly as she raced for the concession stand and the telephone.

She was back in an instant with good news. "She says it's all right, as long as your mother can drive me back. Mrs. Dobkins knows your mother from some club, so there's no problem."

"Good," Lynne said. "My dad'll help us get Dolly into the trailer, and it's just a fifteen-minute ride to the house."

Just as they were about to walk off, Jessie remembered that she had better tell Kate and Dara where she was going. She caught up with them shuffling lethargically out of the stables, and she could see they were feeling crummy about their performances.

"Hi," Jessie said simply, and fell into step beside them. She decided not to discuss the competition.

They responded with friendly enough hellos, and another congratulations to Jessie on her win.

"What're you going to do now?" Jessie asked.

"I'm pretty tired," Dara admitted. "I'm just going to go back and hang out for a while. I think the Dobkinses have a pool."

"Me, too," Kate agreed. "To be honest, I've got a lot on my mind, and I want to have a talk with my horse!"

"Ah, come on," Jessie urged them. "I was hoping you would come with me to visit a girl I met this afternoon who asked me over for a while. She was the one on that neat chestnut bay."

Kate and Dara begged off, and Jessie understood that they were both too upset about their performances to think about being social.

"Well, I guess I'll go ahead and let you two crash," Jessie said. "Catch you later," she hollered back as she ran off to meet Lynne.

It wasn't until later that Jessie realized she had forgotten to tell them she was also going to meet the good-looking boy who had walked away with *their* blue ribbons!

Chapter 3

"YOU live pretty far out in the sticks," Jessie remarked as she took in the view from inside the cab of the Stevenses' old red truck. Jessie, Lynne, and Lynne's father were finally on their way, back to the Stevenses' farm.

"Not really," said Lynne. "We're only ten minutes from town, but we're taking the back roads home to avoid traffic and also because we just like it better, don't we, Dad?"

"You bet," Mr. Stevens agreed. Jessie had a hunch that Lynne and her father were good friends.

"You should see it in the morning," Lynne began, "when the mist comes rolling in over those hills. You can't see but a few feet in front of you, and everything gets sort of dark. The trees look like they're alive. . . ."

"Stop!" Jessie squealed. "You're scaring me."

"The mornings are a little eerie, I guess," Mr. Stevens said, laughing. "I like this time of day, when the light is strong and the view is clear.

Some days you'd think you could see all the way to Canada if you were standing on the top of one of those peaks over there." He pointed to the highest green mountain in the distance.

"Wow," Jessie exclaimed, awed by the vastness of the surroundings.

"Here we are," Lynne said suddenly as they pulled into the next driveway and up to a two-story farmhouse.

"It's beautiful," was Jessie's immediate response as she hopped out of the truck. "You can see for miles around." She turned a complete circle, and surveyed the view.

"We like it here," Lynn said simply. "Mom's inside. You'll meet her as soon as we get Dolly out of her prison. Then we can take her next door to Featherstone Farm, the stable where she boards."

"Great," Jessie said enthusiastically. She had regained her energy after the competition, and now was anxious to see everything.

After unloading a grateful Dolly and meeting Mrs. Stevens, who was every bit as hospitable as her husband, the two girls set off down the road toward Featherstone Farm.

"Dad works for the electric company in Ogden," Lynne informed Jessie as she led Dolly along the shoulder of the road. "I was really lucky to get this horse. Someone was leaving the area, and I guess my parents decided I needed company since I'm an only child, and well ..." Lynne's voice trailed off.

Jessie nodded. She wondered what was coming next.

"Somehow, they found the money to make a down payment on Dolly, and we made arrangements to board her at Featherstone Farm. I couldn't believe it! I'd only had her there a week when they asked me if I wanted a job after school and on weekends cleaning stables and grooming. Wow! Was I relieved. It pays for boarding, and sometimes I make a little extra, which goes toward payments on the horse."

"How old is Dolly?" Jessie asked as she reached to touch the horse's silky mane.

"She's just a baby. Only six years old. And I've had her for about a year and a half now. That's why we're still not perfect in competition. But we'll get there, won't we, Dolly?"

"Darn right," Jessie exclaimed. "She's such a fine-looking mare," Jessie commented, glancing over her fine neck, elegant, small head, and deep girth. She had long, well-angled shoulders, and her coat was shiny and beautiful.

"Such a graceful lady," she added with a chuckle. Dolly did seem to have an aristocractic, well-mannered air about her that made her seem almost dainty.

"You wouldn't say that if you'd seen her when she got out of the paddock last month. She went wild, running all over the place. And she looked like anything but a lady when we tried to round her up and bring her in. You might call her the 'Cher' of the horse world—a combination of devil and angel," Lynne said affectionately. She obviously adored her horse.

Jessie laughed at the reference to Cher. Dolly was so different from her own simple, uncomplicated—and totally dependable—Time-Out.

They turned into a long driveway and began the walk up to Featherstone Farm. The driveway bordered the front paddock, and as they approached the stables they passed several beautiful thoroughbreds. Lynne greeted them all by name, but they didn't even lift their heads, they were so busy chomping on the lush, green grass.

"Humph," said Lynne, as if she were quite insulted. "They actually show off when tourists stop by, but they can't say hello to their groom."

A rambling, three-story brick house stood at the end of the driveway, and another path forked off to the barn and stables in the distance.

"Featherstone is the biggest stable around," said Lynne. "It boards nearly twenty-five horses."

"Twenty-five," Jessie exclaimed, truly impressed. "That must keep the grooms busy."

"You aren't kidding. If I'm not mucking out in real life, I'm doing it in my dreams," Lynne laughed.

The two girls led Dolly into the barn, which was deep enough for eight stalls. Jessie ducked as a barn swallow swooped past her head, and then had to do a quick sidestep to avoid stepping on a frisky calico kitten that came up to greet them.

"Hey, Tortoise!" someone called from inside a stall and then appeared before them. "Watch out!"

The young man bent over and scooped up the little cat and hugged her to his chest.

"You don't stand in the path of horses, do you hear?" He shook his finger at his little friend, and Jessie and Lynne couldn't help but giggle.

"Oh, I'm sorry." The boy seemed a little embarrassed. "This crazy cat's taken to following me around, and I'm afraid that one of these days she's gonna get tromped on."

"Yeah," Jessie agreed, but had to work hard to stop laughing. Geez, she thought helplessly. Why did she always pick the wrong time to get the giggles?

"I'm Ed York," the boy said, extending his hand. "I don't think we've met."

"No. I'm just visiting. I live in Smithfield, Connecticut," Jessie said. The boy was so direct, and so unquestionably cute, she felt shy.

"I saw you this afternoon at the competition," she said, deciding to be brave and plunge into the conversation. "You really did some swell riding. Congratulations."

"Thanks a lot," Ed responded. He actually stopped talking for a long moment to take a good look at Jessie, and it gave her the opportunity to do the same. She had noticed that Ed was quite tall, probably near six feet, and had a great build. He wore his near-black hair a bit long, so that it barely hit the top of the collar on his denim shirt. What she hadn't noticed before were his eyes: enormous and blue like the sky.

"You rode today, too, didn't you?" Thankfully, he had resumed talking.

"Yeah. I'm just Novice, though. You look as if you're ready for the Preliminaries."

Lynne was getting bored with Ed making eyes at Jessie, so she interrupted, "Let's go see if there're oats and water in Dolly's stall, down at the other end of the barn."

Jessie started to follow Lynne, until Ed said, "The horse I was riding is in here." He pointed to a nearby stall. "Wanna see him?"

"Oh, yes." Jessie was definitely interested in

the horse, and she didn't want to leave Ed just yet. She followed him into the stall to take a look at the dappled gray that had made such a hit earlier in the day. It was early evening now, and Ed flicked on a light switch on the wall.

The young gray had a fine composition, a shiny black mane, and tail streaked with silver. His well-muscled hind-quarters and the good bone on his legs spoke of a true champion.

"Prince Hal, meet ..."

"Jessie Robeson," she said to Ed, embarrassed because she hadn't told him her name sooner.

Ed smiled. Lord, Jessie thought, he even has dimples!

"I'm not Prince Hal's owner, though," Ed went on the explain. "His owner is abroad this year, so I've been training him. He said I could enter him today. Prince Hal's a real champion."

Jessie shook her head in agreement.

"I prefer to ride Steeplechase, but I'm going to stick with Prince Hal here and see if we can't do our first three-day event in the spring. Aren't I, boy," Ed spoke affectionately to the horse and then grabbed a brush, and with a few strokes the gray's coat began to gleam.

"I noticed that you won Novice today," Ed turned toward Jessie again. "Congratulations."

"Oh, thanks." She blushed a little. "Time-Out's a good horse."

"Time-Out!" Ed laughed. "What a great name." Something about this response put Jessie at ease. If they could just take it easy on the boy-girl stuff, she knew they could be good friends.

"All set," Lynne said when she returned from

her horse's stall. "Dolly's all bedded down for the
night. She was famished. And come to think of it,
so am I." She stood at the entrance to Prince
Hal's stall, obviously waiting for Jessie.

"Me, too," Jessie affirmed. Inside she felt torn.
A part of her would have loved to stay and talk
more to Ed. But another part of her wanted to get
the heck out of there.

Before she knew it, Ed had resolved her indecision.

"I've got an idea," he said enthusiastically. "Why
don't the two of you come over in the morning
and we'll take the horses for a walk to stretch
their legs after the competition. I was planning to
go out early, and I wouldn't mind some company."

"I don't know . . ." Jessie responded first.

"That means you'd have to sleep over!" Lynne
exclaimed, excited by the idea of an overnight
visit. "Come on, Jessie, it would be neat. We'll get
up when it's still dark and spooky . . ."

"Well, all right." Jessie needed no more convincing. New friends, a different horse to ride . . .
what an adventure! "I'll call the Dobkinses as
soon as we get back to your place, Lynne. I'm
pretty sure they'll say yes."

"All right!" Ed said enthusiastically, and Jessie
could see he really meant it. "Why don't you
come here around six o'clock. I'll try and have
Dolly and a horse for Jessie all saddled."

Jessie was relieved that Lynne also seemed
interested in the plan, because she was in seventh heaven—especially when Mrs. Dobkins immediately gave her permission to stay overnight
at Lynne's. Also, Kate gladly agreed to check on
Time-Out and give her a bran mash that evening.

After she had gobbled down two helpings of an enormous dinner, Jessie sat back in her chair feeling full and fat.

"I am absolutely, positively beat," Lynne exclaimed after finishing off the last bite of her homemade peach pie. "Just thinking about the length of this day makes me tired."

They'd been going nonstop ever since the competition, and Jessie, too, felt as if she were ready to collapse. She couldn't believe they'd promised to be back at the stables by six A.M.!

"You girls do look bushed," Lynne's mother observed. "Your dad will help clean up, so why don't you two go on up to bed."

Lynne dragged herself to her feet, and Jessie followed her up the stairs. It wasn't until they were tucked snugly into bed that Lynne warned Jessie, "I may not make it up in the morning. Waking up that early is not one of the things I do very well."

"Lynne," Jessie squealed in astonishment. "that means I might have to go alone."

"That's right."

Jessie didn't think long about the connotation of Lynne's reply, because the very next moment she was fast asleep. When the alarm went off at 5:30 A.M. she couldn't believe it was morning already. Her entire body felt like lead, and her heavy head seemed permanently glued to the pillow.

Jessie looked over at Lynne sleeping in the twin bed next to her. She had let the alarm ring for a while after it went off, but even so, Lynne didn't stir.

"Lynne ..." Jessie gently prodded her shoulder. "It's time to get up."

Lynne opened her eyes a crack and said, "I don't feel so good, Jessie. You'd better go without me." She rolled over to go back to sleep and then added, "You can ride Dolly."

Jessie was surprised that Lynne wasn't going, and she couldn't help but wonder if Lynne had noticed that Ed seemed to like her, and had deliberately decided to stay home.

I don't have time to worry about why she's not coming, Jessie concluded as she raced down the road in the still-dark morning to Featherstone Farm.

Ed was ready and waiting when Jessie arrived. Both Dolly and Prince Hal were already saddled. Ed was just throwing a saddle pad trimmed in gold and green, the stable's colors, on the third horse, when Jessie sprinted into the barn.

"You don't have to saddle her," she said breathlessly. "Lynne's not feeling well and didn't come."

"Good," Ed answered spontaneously, then retracted his remark. "I don't mean good that she's not coming. I mean good that I don't have to saddle another horse." He looked a little embarrassed by his impulsive response.

Jessie smiled. It was almost as if Lynne and Ed had the whole thing planned, she thought, as she approached Dolly and spoke to her softly so she wouldn't be afraid when Jessie mounted her.

"How're the stirrups?" Ed asked before he jumped up on Prince Hal.

"Just right, I think," Jessie said. He'd made a good guess about her height.

Moments later they were moving slowly and tentatively along the trail, poking giant holes through clouds of heavy mist that hung in the air in front of them. Jessie understood now why Lynne had said that the gnarled trees reminded her of strange, hoary old monsters with a million arms and wrinkly, knotted faces.

"It's really something," Jessie exclaimed.

"Yeah," he hollered back. The initial section of the trail cut through dense woods, and they had to walk single file along the narrow path. "Mornings on this mountain are really special."

Then, suddenly, they rode out into a beautiful clearing, and the first sliver of sunlight peeked up and over the far horizon.

"Good morning," Ed said when Jessie rode up beside him.

"The same to you," she responded, glad that the trail was finally wide enough so they could ride side by side and talk.

"Hey, sleepyhead," Ed said after staring at her for a moment. "I don't think you're even awake yet."

"Just barely," Jessie admitted.

"I was surprised you made it at all," Ed said, and smiled warmly. After a few minutes of silently enjoying the view, he continued, "What's it like in Smithfield, anyway, Jess?"

"Oh, I don't know," Jessie began. He had already used her nickname! "When I'm not in school or doing chores at home, I'm usually at Windcroft Stables where I work and train my horse."

"I can just see it now," Ed said with a faraway look in his eyes. "Someday I'll pick up the paper and there you'll be: TIME-OUT AND JESSIE, OLYMPIC CHAMPIONS."

"Oh, sure," Jessie replied. Ed was treading on sensitive ground.

"Seriously, Jessie. I mean, I don't know that much myself, but I think if you can find a way to keep training—and training hard—you may even be on your way to the Olympics."

In Jessie's heart of hearts she was soaring. She knew that the most important ingredient for getting there was to believe in herself, but it sure was good to hear someone else say he believed in her. She liked Ed and he seemed to like her, and at this moment, on this fresh and sparkling morning, Jessie felt like she had everything she ever wanted.

Basking in the intensity of her joy, Jessie urged Dolly into a smooth canter and moved a couple of strides ahead of Ed. "Hurry up, slowpoke." She turned and flashed him a bright smile. "I want to see what's up ahead. . . ."

Chapter 4

"My Lady," Kate and Dara addressed Jessie in unison. They stood side by side and bowed formally, gesturing toward the cab of the van.

"Stop it! You're embarrassing me." Jessie giggled.

"No," said Dara quite seriously. "It's only fair. "The blue ribbon winner deserves the middle seat."

"Does that mean I'll get the royal treatment all the way home?" The idea began to appeal to Jessie.

"No," Kate declared. "It means that Time-Out will get an extra big helping of mash when *she* gets home."

Kate and Dara jumped up into the van beside Jessie, leaving just enough room for their driver. Jessie enjoyed the fun of pig-piling it to a show, especially when she was with her best friends. On the other hand, when Anne came along, they had the luxury of riding in the station wagon, and could even lie down in the back and sleep.

"All set then?" Mr. Tucker asked when the girls seemed reasonably settled.

"Yes," they chorused, and with a roar of the engine and a grinding of gears, they were off, headed back to Windcroft.

"It seems as if we've been gone forever," Jessie remarked, suddenly excited about the idea of going home.

"Longer for you than for us," Dara retorted as she kicked off her loafers and tried to get comfortable for the first lap of the four-hour ride. "You didn't see Kate and me off gallivanting all over the countryside last night."

"Big deal," Jessie feigned a sophisticated tone. "I simply decided to spend a night out with a new friend, since my traveling companions were so tired they had to go home. Ogden, of course, is a very happening town."

"Yeah, we know," Kate responded. "The most exciting place in Ogden must be the local Dairy Queen."

"By the way," Dara said. "How is the ice cream in Massachusetts? Are the ice-cream scoopers anything like Amory?"

"Dara Cooper, if you ever mention his name again in front of me I'm going to kill you!" Jessie screamed, and flailed her fists in the air until she caught an annoyed "pipe down" look from Mr. Tucker.

Mr. Tucker's silent reprimand started a giggling fit that took several minutes to control.

Kate made the mistake of asking "Hey, what the heck is so funny?" And they began to laugh even harder.

"All right," Dara finally managed to squeak out as she wiped a tear from her eye. "I won't mention Amory again. There's no more mileage in that one."

For a few moments they sat in silence, catching their breath. Then Kate piped up, "Jessie told me there might be a new man in her life, didn't you, Jess? Come on, tell us everything."

Dara slid forward to the edge of the seat and said, "Out with it, Jessie. Who is he? What happened?"

Jessie deliberately glanced out the window, keeping her friends in suspense, so when she finally did tell them about Ed, they hung on every word.

"Ohhh," Dara moaned in agony. She tugged at the roots of her short blond hair as if she wanted to pull it out. "I can't stand it. There must be some mistake here. I knew the minute I saw him that that dreamboat was meant for me."

"Well, it didn't happen this time, hotshot," Jessie declared. Dara was so sophisticated and pretty, often she was the one the boys noticed first.

"What about Doug?" Jessie raised her eyebrows. She was a little surprised that she already felt slightly possessive of Ed.

"Yeah," Kate supported Jessie. She gave Dara a gentle poke of the elbow. "What about Doug, you little flirt?"

"Oh, yes, Doug," Dara said languidly. "Well, my mother taught me to always shop around. After all, you never know when you might find a better model."

With that remark, the mood in the van again went from silly to downright hysterical. After the exciting weekend, everyone was tired—and slap-happy. But after a while, when they crossed the state line into Connecticut, Kate got serious again. "Jessie, do you think you'll see him again?"

"I don't know," Jessie answered, suddenly missing Ed—and her new friend Lynne, too. "He said he was going to write me," she told them, and privately crossed her fingers in hope.

"We'll stop here for gas and a bite to eat," Mr. Tucker informed them as he pulled into the parking lot of a truck stop and restaurant. "Better see that the horses still have water," he suggested before hopping out.

Although the horses were fine, it was obvious from their impatient whinnies that all three would prefer to have been let out and given a booth and a bucket of sweet feed alongside the girls, who gobbled down sandwiches and cold drinks.

"Only an hour and a half to go," Jessie said when they got back in the van and Mr. Tucker drove back onto the highway. For the millionth time they began to rehash the competition, and talk about what went right—and what went wrong.

"I guess my work's cut out for me when I get home," Kate said. "I'm going to have to work Spy extra-long for a couple of days and figure out just where we aren't clicking."

"It's just a little miscommunication, I think," Jessie interjected. "After all, you haven't been riding him for very long."

Kate agreed. "He's just got to learn who's boss." She paused to reflect for a moment. "But at least he's keen to go. No cross-country course will ever stop that horse," she concluded.

"I knew the competition would be rough, but I didn't expect that gray—or your boyfriend—to walk away with the ribbon." Dara directed her remark to Jessie.

"Ah, come on, Dara," Kate said. "You were distracted again. I saw it. The same thing happened to you last time." Kate stopped suddenly, hoping she hadn't been too blunt with her friend.

"I know," Dara admitted. "No excuses. I hate to admit it; it's so idiotic. I don't think I warmed Arpeggio up enough before his dressage. Something told me his muscles were a little tight as soon as we made the first circle, and that broke my concentration. There's nothing wrong with the horse," she went on dejectedly. "It's the rider who's screwing up." Dara looked absolutely miserable.

"Ah, Dara," Jessie tried to comfort her. "Don't be too hard on yourself. It's just one little show, after all. Besides, because of Arpeggio's injury and time off, you should be darn proud of your third-place ribbon."

It didn't take long before the two friends had cajoled Dara back into a good mood. Then the focus turned to Jessie.

"Jessie, you were tops," Dara said affectionately. "We were truly proud of you."

Kate nodded her agreement, "I wonder if your name's going to be in the next *Chronicle*."

"It better be," Dara chimed in, "and a picture, too." She grabbed a yellow sweatshirt from behind the seat and pulled it over her head. The fall afternoons were getting cooler.

"Speaking of pictures, do you think we oughta tell her?" Kate smiled mischievously.

"I don't know," Dara said. "Do you really think she deserves it?"

"Nah, we might as well wait till we get home," Kate teased.

"Tell me right now!" Jessie demanded. "Come on, tell me." She could barely control herself.

"Well ..." Kate looked at Dara and said, "You tell her."

"Well," Dara began, "don't be surprised if you get a package in the mail within a couple of weeks from the official photographer of the Ogden Combined Training Competition."

"Photographer!" Jessie said in disbelief.

"Yep. We hired him to take pictures of you and Time-Out after we saw that you were going to win. It's our present to a worthy friend."

Jessie was so touched she thought she was going to cry. She would have a real memento from the weekend. Something to show her family ...

"I saw him shooting you during presentations, and you looked great," Dara said. "Time-Out was alert and standing perfectly square, and you looked simply smashing."

"Oh." Jessie fell back into her seat, overwhelmed. Then she turned around once more and said, shyly, "Thanks, guys. I don't get a chance to tell you this often, but—"

"Yuck," Kate said, making a face. "None of that gushy stuff, thank you."

Dara, who was obviously pleased to have made Jessie happy, simply sat back and smiled.

The moment they pulled into the driveway at Windcroft Stables, Anne came running out of the house to greet them. Kate had already called her and told her about the results of the competition, but she quizzed them all again as they unloaded the horses from the van and walked them around the training ring a few turns before getting them into their stalls for the night.

Normally Jessie would have also put Time-Out in her stall, but she was feeling especially proud of her after Anne's effusive praise, so she decided to let her stay out for the night as a special treat. After all, the weather was good, and there was room in the paddock. Jessie dragged a bale of hay from the barn to the fence and stood on tiptoe to throw a couple of flakes to her beloved horse. Then she put extra shavings in Time-Out's stall so that when she did come in the following morning, she would be clean and comfortable.

The autumn air was crisp and cool, and the setting sun sailed swiftly across a golden sky. In another hour it would be dark.

"Don't you want to come in and have some dessert?" Anne asked Dara and Jessie.

"Sure," Dara responded enthusiastically. "Come on." She grabbed Jessie's arm.

But Jessie shook her head, saying, "No. I can't. I'm late as it is. My father expected me home a couple of hours ago. I can ride my bicycle." She pointed to her bike, which was leaning against the barn, just where she had left it.

On the ride home Jessie felt an excitement churn up inside her, and she realized how anxious she was to get there. She hadn't given her family a second thought in three days, but now as she neared the house she had lived in almost all her life, she became aware of how much she loved it—and everyone in it.

"I'm home," she yelled, letting the screen door slam behind her.

"We're in here," she heard Sarah call from the kitchen. Jessie put her knapsack down on the bench in the back hallway, and ran to the kitchen to say hello.

She could hardly believe her eyes when she saw her brother Nick leaning over the sink, actually doing dishes. Sarah was there alongside him, standing in a little pool of water, drying.

Jessie's first impulse was to laugh, but then she realized that the mood was anything but cheerful. For starters, Nick hated doing any kind of housework, and in the past had always been excused to run errands like shopping or mailing letters instead.

"Dad hurt his back," was all Nick said.

Jessie couldn't believe the look he gave her. As if it were all *her* fault.

Sarah continued with the explanation. "We had this big storm on Saturday night and a tree fell across the top of the garage. Dad was trying to lift it off, and it was too heavy. He had to go to the gyropractor," she finished, breathless.

"Chiropractor, stupid," Nick said. His mood was definitely foul.

"He's in there," Sarah offered, nodding toward the living room.

Alarmed, Jessie raced into the next room and saw her father stretched out in an awkward position on the old flowered couch.

He peered up at her. A clipped "hello" was his only greeting.

"Dad! What happened?" Jessie inquired.

"I guess you already heard," he said in a soft, steady voice, as if he were trying to move as little as possible. Even the subtle motion involved in talking threatened to jar him back into pain. "I just sprained my back. I'll be fine in a couple of days."

"Oh, Dad," Jessie said with compassion. She knelt down beside him, but was scared to touch him. "I'm so sorry. You should have called me. I'd have come home sooner."

"Forget it," her father cut her short. "We managed okay. And besides, I didn't want to spoil your fun. ..."

"Oh," was all Jessie could say. Then, "Is there anything I can do for you?"

"No. Just make sure Nick and Sarah are ready for school tomorrow." He adjusted his position on the couch, and his face contorted in pain. "If your mother were here ..." The words slipped out of his mouth.

Jessie could hardly keep from crying. What would her mother do, her mind raced, if she were here? As much as she tried to be like her mother, she certainly could never replace her. In fact, the idea was preposterous. But her father's words made Jessie feel terrible that she hadn't been there when he needed her.

Jessie felt hot tears spring to her eyes as she ran up the stairs to her room. It was bad enough coming home to such a mess. But worse yet was that no one had even bothered to ask her about the competition. ...

Chapter 5

SPLASHES of red sumac and yellow elms had begun to break up the dense green foliage that surrounded Windcroft, and the stables looked like the center of a vibrant bouquet displaying the beauty and wonder of autumn. The air was crisp and clean, and a gentle breeze turned a corner and sneaked into the barn, tickling the horses and making them feel frisky and playful.

"Easy, boy," Jessie cooed as she opened the door to E.T.'s stall, carrying a pail of half pellets and half oats. "That's right. Just relax. I've got your food, and you're gonna get it if you'll kindly move aside and let me in."

Jessie continued a quiet dialogue with the horse, hoping that he would behave. A real space cadet, she thought, remembering how for his first six months at the stable it had been impossible to even get past him to fill his food bucket. He was so overanxious to eat, he would plunge his head into the pail and wouldn't take it out, so they couldn't dispense his feed. For the past few months, the only thing that worked was to go into the stall with a crop; a language he seemed to understand. Not that Jessie ever used it. It was just a question of letting him know that if he pushed people, they pushed back.

"You boarders. I wonder who trained you, anyway," Jessie sighed.

E.T. was now wolfing down his feed at an incredibly rapid—and noisy—pace. In contrast to him, Anne's horses were so well-mannered that given a simple command—"Down"—they would lower their heads to be bridled. "Got to get you civilized," was Jessie's final word as she hooked the lock on E.T.'s door.

Jessie moved to the next stall and said hello to Bebe, the thirty-six year-old pony that the Wileys had owned since Kate had first started to ride. In fact, Kate's initial involvement with horses had started when she fell in love with Bebe. "Hey, little girl," Jessie greeted her warmly. The pony rubbed her nose against Jessie's shoulder in an affectionate hello. "Here's your sweet feed," Jessie announced. "And I'm going to get you a fresh pail of nice, cold water."

Because of her age, Bebe had recently been having trouble with her teeth, and sometimes it was difficult for her to chew hay. She had no problems with softened pellets, however, which she hungrily devoured. Before going on to the next stall, Jessie reached up and gave Bebe a little hug and whispered "I love you" to her aging friend.

Jessie was just about to go on to Caesar,

named of course for his Roman nose, when she heard Anne call her from outside the barn.

"Coming," she answered, and turned to the hungry horse. "You'll just have to wait, Mr. C.," Jessie informed him, much to his obvious dismay.

"Jessie," Anne said when she approached her. "Can you stop for a second? I'd like to talk to you."

"Oh, sure," said Jessie, surprised by the unusual visit. "I was going to tell you we should order some more hay right away. We're almost down to the bad bales we were going to save for mulch in the spring."

"So soon!" Anne looked surprised.

"Yes. A lot of that last load was moldy in the center, so I didn't feed it to the horses."

"Good," Anne said approvingly. She and Jessie walked outside together as they talked. Jessie leaned against the barn and Anne stood a short distance away, facing her. Feeling a little as if she were cornered, Jessie sensed she was in a for a heavy conversation.

"As a matter of fact," Anne went on, "I recently decided that I've been long overdue in telling you that I think you're doing a superb job for us here, and that I was very proud of you and Time-Out for bringing home that blue ribbon. You've shown us you've got real talent," she added.

"Oh, I don't know." Jessie cast her eyes down and toed the ground. She felt flattered, but also embarrassed.

"I want you to come in the house after you're done today and we'll talk about giving you a little raise for your work around here. Also," Anne continued. "I want you to have this."

Jessie hadn't noticed the garment that Anne had been carrying under her arm. She was shocked when she saw that it was the handsome black dressage jacket she had borrowed for the show.

"Oh, I couldn't," Jessie stammered. At the same time, she was simply dying to take it.

"I know, dear," Anne responded, "you're going to feel a little funny about it. But the truth is, I think I'm finally approaching what is known as the 'middle-aged spread.' Another year and it won't even fit. I really would like you to have it." She held out the coat to Jessie.

"Well ..." Jessie hesitated a moment longer and then accepted the gift. "Oh, thank you," she said profusely, hugging the coat to her chest. "I just ... I just love it! And I'm sure it will always bring me luck."

Anne was very pleased by Jessie's reaction and was about to go back to the house, leaving Jessie to finish up the afternoon feeding. But instead she resumed their conversation.

"So"—her effort to sound casual didn't quite work—"other than your job here, how are things going for you, Jessie?"

"Fine, I guess." A lie, Jessie thought instantly. Inside, she could feel herself starting to clam up.

"Everything okay at home ... and at school?" Anne continued to probe.

"Yeah, I guess so." Except that I've always got so much work to do I feel like I've been sentenced to Sing Sing, Jessie thought. She really didn't feel like telling Anne what she was thinking. Or anyone else, for that matter. After all, who was she to complain? It was her choice to be involved with horses.

But somehow Anne managed to catch her gaze, and she stared into Jessie's hazel eyes looking for the truth. Feeling as if she had been caught red-handed, Jessie immediately came clean. If anyone could get her to open up, it was Anne. "I guess I have been feeling a little low on energy lately."

"Is it because you've been working too hard?" Anne asked.

"Oh, it isn't that." Jessie squirmed. She hated talking about herself, and especially about her problems.

"I *love* working Spy in the mornings. It's just all the other stuff I have to do at home." Feeling awkward, she spoke softly, so Anne moved closer to her. "The housekeeper quit, so there's no one to help with the chores now. And Dad hurt his back while I was gone."

Then, suddenly, the truth gushed out. "I just wish Mom were still here." As soon as she said it, Jessie felt both deeply distraught—and at the same time relieved. How important it was to share!

"I know." Anne's voice was thick with compassion. She stepped forward and put an arm around Jessie's shoulders and gave her a long, supportive hug. "I've often thought how strong you are, going through what you did. And now, with all your responsibilities at home ..."

Jessie was determined not to cry. Instead, she swallowed her tears and let herself be hugged until she felt better.

"Well," Anne said after a few moments. "I think you definitely need to get some help at home as soon as possible. It's not fair for you to go on like this too much longer. Do you think your father—"

Jessie quickly interrupted her. "Oh, please don't say anything to my father," she begged. "He's got so many worries of his own now. I know that money is a problem, and he's trying to get better so he can go back to work full-time."

Anne still looked concerned.

"I know he's going to get someone soon," Jessie tried to convince her. "I can do it for a little while longer, and I do so want to help him. After all, he and Grandma bought Time-Out for me."

Anne stepped back again and took a long, final look at her.

"Maybe for a few more weeks," she said. Now that Jessie had confided in her, Anne had the right to a real say in her problems. "But I'm going to ask you about it again soon, and if things haven't changed and you're still looking so tired, I just might play Ms. Buttinsky and talk to your father."

Whew! Jessie felt relieved. Anne started back to the house and Jessie turned back to the barn to finish feeding the horses, thinking about how grown-up she always felt after one of these wonderfully wretched conversations.

After she had finished up her chores at Windcroft —which included a phone call to schedule an appointment with Willy, the farrier, to come the next week because three horses had thrown shoes—Jessie raced home. She had recently started making use of the freezer by cooking lots on weekends and simply reheating things during the week. Since her father had called to say he was going to be late, it was just Nick, Sarah, and Jessie who gobbled up the tuna casserole and salad as ravenously as the horses had attacked their feed.

"Let me see it again, please," Sarah pleaded later on, when the dishes were done and they were in their room. Instead of studying, Jessie was lying on her bed examining the photo she had received that day in the mail of herself and Time-Out in Ogden. The photographer must have been a magician, she thought, admiring the shot. Time-Out, indeed, stood alert and square, clearly a fine example of her breed.

"Even your old sister looks pretty good here," she kidded as she handed the photo to Sarah. But before Sarah could take it, Jessie pulled it back and asked, "Are your hands clean?"

"Yes," said Sarah impatiently. She took the picture and climbed up on her bed, where she sat cross-legged, examining it.

"Wow, you look beautiful," Sarah exclaimed proudly. "I never knew you were so pretty."

"Oh, Sarah," Jessie exclaimed modestly. But her sister's remark provoked her to go to the vanity and take a good look at herself.

Jessie had been so busy lately that she rarely stopped to look in a mirror. Now, as she carefully inspected her image, she saw that her hair had grown a good inch during the summer. She definitely needed a trim. Her face was a trifle gaunt, and as she gazed briefly into her eyes she thought she somehow looked older and much more mature than she did last year. Jessie still loved the kelly green cardigan with leather elbows she now wore over a pale yellow blouse, but she could see by the slightly frayed collar and missing top button that it was getting near its end. Remembering that she had worn it the morning she went riding with Ed, she vowed that when they did get together again, she would wear something new.

"Can't I take it to school?" Sarah interrupted her thoughts. "The kids will die when I show them."

"No. Definitely not," Jessie said sternly as she reached for the photo. For a moment it seemed as if Sarah might not give it up. "You can't carry a photograph all over the place. It'll get ruined. You can take the ribbon to show the class instead."

"Ah, they already saw the first one," Sarah complained, but then perked up. "But are they ever gonna be jealous when they hear you won another."

Jessie was about to explain to Sarah that winning anything wasn't about jealousy or making other people feel bad, but just then her father tapped lightly on the bedroom door.

"Hello, girls," he said with a weak smile. He walked over to Sarah and patted her cheek. "About time for you to get to bed, isn't it?"

Sarah's expression reflected fierce opposition to the idea, but she got up immediately and went to her drawer for her pajamas, resigned to her eight-year-old's fate.

"Can I talk to you for a minute downstairs?" her father asked Jessie. As she followed him down the steps and into the kitchen, Jessie realized this was the second time today that she was summoned into what looked like serious conversation. Only this time, she was scared.

"One of the reasons I'm late is because I had a visit with Roger after work," her father began. They sat at a table in the pale blue kitchen, a cozy room that still held tantalizing smells from the night's dinner. Only one dim wall light remained on, and Jessie couldn't see her father's face very clearly. But since Roger Silverman, her advanced algebra teacher, also happened to be one of Mr. Robeson's best friends, she could only cringe and guess what was to come.

"Jess," Mr. Robeson got right to the point, "he told me your grades are slipping. Is that true?" His tone of voice was quite serious.

Jessie squirmed in her chair and chewed on the edge of a ragged fingernail. There was no way she could deny it. "Maybe. A little bit. But they're bound to get better.

"That's not what I hear," said her father. There was more. "I hear you got a D on your last test. That's unheard of for you. You're a straight A student."

"I know," Jessie said weakly. "But math is a hard subject for me. I did okay in geometry last year, but algebra and trig are hopeless."

"Well, the only way I know to 'get' it is to start studying, pronto," declared Mr. Robeson.

Jessie sat quietly, gazing at her clenched fingers. Her insides were in a turmoil, and her cheeks felt hot. She begged herself not to get angry.

"Well. Are you just going to sit there?" her

father wanted to know. He raised his voice. "Don't you have anything at all to say?"

"I don't know what to say," Jessie said miserably. "I'm doing well in all my other subjects, but it's just that I hate algebra." She stopped to take a breath.

"Maybe I *would* do better If I studied more." She paused, and then blurted out, a bit too belligerently, "But I'd like to know when I have the time?"

"I know it's been hard on you, with Mrs. Mc-Pherson gone and all," her father began on a note of understanding, but it quickly dissolved when he started getting angry. "But that's no excuse. You know that I'm planning to look for someone else soon, and that your responsibilities around here are just temporary. I think the problem just might be the horse."

As soon as she heard the words, Jessie froze. She was terrified at the thought of what was coming next.

"I hear you getting up at five-thirty in the morning to go over to those stables, and most nights you don't get back until five thirty or six o'clock. When we agreed to get you the horse, Jessie, I never dreamed she would take over your life."

"She hasn't ..." Jessie tried to interrupt.

"She has!" her father insisted, pounding his fist on the table.

He seemed to her like a different person— someone she had never met before. For the second time that day she felt hot tears well up in her eyes. Only this time, she had no defense. Her father was at the point where he simply wouldn't listen to her.

"Young lady, I only have one thing to say." He stood up to issue his severe verdict. "From now on, you're going to have to change your priorities. Until I see that your math grades are improving, there'll be no more going over to Windcroft before school. You can do your two hours of afternoon work there, but that's it. I want you home Sunday afternoons, too. Studying."

"Ah, Dad," Jessie just couldn't bear it. She rested her heavy head in her hands and felt a dull ache in her stomach.

"It's not going to help to 'ah, Dad,' me," Mr. Robeson assured her. "The situation is serious and *I'm* serious. If this solution doesn't work, you won't be riding that horse at all. Because you'll be permanently grounded."

Chapter 6

"YOUR turn, Time-Out. Let's go," Jessie instructed her horse with a slight nudge of her leg. Time-Out immediately extended her pace and stepped out of the line of trotting horses to pass Arpeggio and Spy. She then took her position as leader about fifty feet ahead of the others.

"Good girl," Jessie reinforced Time-Out's correct performance. They slowed down a bit to let the others catch up.

It was Saturday, and Jessie and her friends had finished with their individual lessons with Anne. Now they were trotting along a back trail, working together on cross-country. Since it was especially crisp that autumn afternoon, Kate and Dara wore heavy sweaters, and Jessie, her red plaid wool vest.

It was now Arpeggio's turn to move up to the front, and Jessie could hear Dara giving the command.

"Whoa," Kate said with authority when Spy

became inattentive and then tried to race and catch up to Arpeggio. One of the reasons they were spending so much time on this exercise was to help cure Spy of rushing. If he were allowed to have this way, he would simply take off, and to heck with obedience. When a horse tried to pass him, he thought he was being left behind, so he just chugged along.

"Good boy," Kate reinforced when he responded to her commands to stay in line.

After continuing the exercise for several more rounds, they came to the edge of the woods and into a clearing, and they paused for a moment to rest. "Sure is pretty," Dara remarked as she stopped for a look at the panoramic sky. It was hard not to appreciate the colors of autumn in Connecticut.

"Would you mind if we rode down to the meadow now?" Kate pointed ahead to the clearing in which several clumps of small scrub pines were growing. "Since I've got you two to help me, I'd like to do some work with Spy."

Jessie and Dara were happy to oblige. When they got to the other side of the meadow, the two girls got off their horses and dragged a cavalletti out from where it was hidden at the edge of the trees. They placed it almost smack in the center of a clump of pines, and then each girl held the trees apart at the side of the jump to make an opening in the middle.

"Ready," Jessie signaled Kate. Spy approached and cleared the jump and all the brush with ease.

"Roll it over so it's medium height," Kate said. "I want him to brush through the trees when he steps over the cavalletti." She turned Spy around and he again made the jump with no effort.

"I guess you must wonder what we're doing." Kate patted Spy's neck. Getting used to walking through pines was something Spy hadn't learned when he was younger. Left on his own, he would probably just continue to sail over the tops of the trees and waste energy, not a good idea for a three-day eventer. So they had to take their time and do several trial runs with Dara and Jessie holding the scrubs apart before Spy agreed to walk through the pines, and discover the prickly branches that brushed his legs weren't hairy monsters, and a little contact with nature wouldn't hurt him.

"Thanks," Kate said to her friends when they had gone back and forth a few times. "I think he's finally beginning to get the idea."

"I think so, too," said Jessie, understanding Spy's confusion. "All he needs is some retraining."

Dara had found a path skirting the edge of the meadow with low-hanging overhead branches that made flowery patterns of light and dark against the yellow-green grass and perfectly simulated a portion of the trail in the last competition. Arpeggio was sometimes hesitant going into the dark, so Dara took advantage of the situation and spent the next few minutes practicing serpentines, weaving in and out of the shadows. She stayed in the dark just long enough for his eyes to dilate so when they stepped back into the dazzling sunlight, Arpeggio would get used to those few seconds of blindness.

As for Time-Out, Jessie was feeling good about

her practice that day. Earlier they had also worked over cavallettis with Anne. They ended with bounce jumps over water, and Time-Out was comfortable and confident. Jessie was glad she seemed to be getting over her dislike for anything wet. In fact, Time-out was becoming a regular puddle duck from Jessie's unrelenting insistence that they go through every little pool of water, to teach the horse that these puddles really weren't deep, dark holes leading all the way to China.

Horses, like people, have their own special variety of fears and hang-ups, Jessie thought as she stood watching Dara and Arpeggio.

"Well, how's it going?" Kate inquired as they reunited again in the center of the clearing.

"Fine," said Jessie, "but I think we should call it a day. I'm hungry."

"You're always hungry." Dara smiled as she toyed with the buckle that joined her reins. "Keep eating so much and one day Time-Out'll be riding you."

"Very funny," retorted Jessie. "I wouldn't talk. You're the one who consumes a gallon of ice cream every two days."

"Tonight we're having spaghetti," Kate announced. "And salad, and Italian bread, and apple pie—à la mode."

"Oh, man. I can't wait!" sang out Jessie. It was Saturday night and she and Dara were sleeping at Kate's. It was their first bona fide pajama party in a long time. She never thought she could talk her father into letting her stay, but he finally agreed when Jessie promised to spend the next day helping with the yardwork.

"Last one back's a . . ." Jessie stopped to think.

"Last one back has to do the dishes," Kate announced, knowing that Spy could beat the other two home.

As it turned out, Dara was the last to return to the stables, and she walked in slowly. Since her accident with Arpeggio, she didn't like galloping her horse. "I'm not interested in racing, you know that," she said as she dismounted.

"Oh, Dara. What a drag. You know we wouldn't take any chances with the horses over a little thing like seeing who can get home first. We don't go very fast, and besides, once in a while a person's gotta have a little fun."

"She has her fun with Doug," Jessie chimed in, "riding around in his car listening to country-western songs."

"Oh, yeah? Here's another way I have fun!" Dara ran over and grabbed the hose that happened to be on because the groom was sponging the horses.

Kate and Jessie could be heard squealing all the way to the next county as Dara gave them both a good bath.

"Now. Who are you calling a drag?" She laughed.

"No one," Kate backed off.

"Not you," Jessie assured her. After all, Dara was still holding the hose, a rather formidable weapon.

"Truce," they all agreed instantly and the three friends strolled arm in arm back toward the house.

After their scrumptious dinner Dara and Kate shared kitchen cleanup duty while Jessie went out to check the horses and cover Time-Out.

She couldn't resist giving her a quick grooming. Time-Out always seemed to appreciate a brush, and Jessie wanted all of her hair lying smooth before covering her with a blue plaid Baker blanket that would keep her nice and toasty during the cool fall night. Also, Jessie hoped that by blanketing Time-Out early, she might be able to stunt the growth of her coat so she would only need one clipping in the spring.

"Good night, My Lady," Jessie said to Time-Out, fluffing up her shavings. There wouldn't be any time the next day to ride her, and Jessie knew she would miss their usual Sunday afternoon stroll. "Don't worry," Jessie promised Time-Out, "I'm not going anywhere. I'll be back on Monday."

By the time Jessie returned to the house, Kate and Dara had already finished cleaning up the kitchen and were up in Kate's room. Jessie ran upstairs to join them, and found her friends sitting in their pajamas on their beds, talking about the next competition.

Jessie grabbed her overnight case and went into the bathroom to change into her nightshirt and brush her teeth. She kept the door ajar so she could hear what Kate and Dara were saying.

"I just can't wait till November," Dara exclaimed, "when we go to Windsor." Jessie knew she was referring to the upcoming fall competition at the Windsor House Horse Trials. "I can picture us now, pulling into that long driveway to the estate and parking the van at the end of that incredible alfalfa field," Dara mused.

"Yeah," Kate interjected. "I remember that edible parking lot. It took me half an hour to drag Night Owl out of there. He loves alfalfa."

The girls giggled as Jessie finished washing up and plopped up onto her bed, ready to join in.

"What I couldn't believe was the size of those stalls," Jessie said, "and that incredible security system. Television cameras in the barn! No way anyone could walk off with one of those horses."

"I remember the stone mansion." Kate's eyes had a faraway, dreamy look as she recalled the fifty-room main house on the Windsor estate that was surrounded by huge elm trees hundreds of years old. "And those cast iron and mahogany saddle racks in the tack room."

"Yeah," Jessie confirmed wistfully. The memory was coming into focus.

The Windsor House Horse Trials were traditionally held twice a year, once in November and again in the spring, and last year Jessie had been fortunate enough to be able to go with Kate and Dara for an entire week of precompetition training. The girls had been able to school over the fences for three days before the competition.

The Windsor course was considered the best in the Northeast. All the fences were made of sturdy timber, and there were no deceiving ground lines. The jumps also were all well-placed and had good footing, and Jessie remembered one in particular that was a miniature tabletop set into a stone wall with two little chairs on either side. There were beautiful perennial flowers around the permanent dressage ring, and an enormous grass warm-up area.

"I don't care what I have to do," Dara stood up and declared dramatically. "If they have the three-day after horse trials, I can't miss it."

"Sit down, dummy," Kate teased. "The three-day is going to be in the spring, like last year. I'm sure we'll be able to go back to see them. We should be grateful we can go at all!"

"By the way," Dara addressed Jessie, ignoring Kate's little scolding, "won't your new boyfriend be in the Preliminary level?" It was perhaps Dara who loved the Windsor competition more than any of them, and the mere thought of the upcoming show made her giddy with excitement.

"Come to think of it, I guess he will." Jessie blushed. She hadn't yet started thinking of Ed as her boyfriend. But still, there was the letter. ...

Jessie had reluctantly shown Kate and Dara the letter she had gotten from Ed the day before. Or, more appropriately, they had pried it out of her. Jessie had already written Lynne twice, and they had become fast friends. But this was the first time she had heard from Ed since the event in Ogden, and she had to admit, she was outrageously happy to have received it.

Dear Jessie—she remembered it word-for-word— *A quick note to say hello from all of the beasties at Featherstone Farm—including me. Lynne and I keep talking about how much fun it was when you were here.*"

Ed had gone on to tell her a little bit about what he was doing this fall, and to describe his school. Then he had ended just as affectionately as he had begun, giving Jessie—and Kate and

Dara—the definite feeling that he might have romantic plans for the future:

I still remember that morning we rode together, and how glad I was when I saw you coming up the path alone. I knew then I'd have a chance to get to know you. Which I did. Well enough to know how much I want to see you—and Time-Out—again. For your information, Jessie, even though we live far apart, I'm going to try and make that happen. I hope you agree, and also want to be good friends. Or more, Jessie hoped.

"Come to think of it, I'm pretty sure Ed will have made Preliminary three-day by next spring," Jessie announced, suddenly confident about her relationship with him and optimistic about the future.

"This year we'll have to be sure and buy tickets for ringside seats and take a picnic lunch," Kate declared, "instead of staking out standing room like we did last year."

"Who cares about spring," Dara spoke up. "I'm just worried about now. November is right around the corner, you know."

Kate, suddenly alert, sat up on her bed, feet tucked underneath her. She drew her light paisley quilt around her shoulders for warmth. "You're right, Dara. It really isn't very far off."

"I think I've talked my parents into giving me my new dressage saddle before Christmas, for the competition," Dara announced, and both Kate and Jessie applauded her shrewd success. Competing at Windsor definitely warranted a new saddle.

Still, Kate had her own priorities when it came

to the show. "I really don't care if I have a new saddle or not. I just want Spy to be relaxed."

"Let's see," Kate continued, "If we leave here on Tuesday night, we'll have all of Wednesday, Thursday, and Friday to school the horses before the competition."

"That means, counting Monday, we'll only miss four days of school," Dara said. "No one's going to get bent out of shape about that."

"I'm not so sure ..." Jessie murmured, getting back into the conversation. Her dejected tone of voice immediately caught her friends' attention.

"You are going, aren't you?" Kate immediately deciphered Jessie's hesitation.

When she still didn't answer, Dara jumped in. "The three of us are a team, remember? And we all know that if you make a splash at Windsor in Novice, you'll definitely move up to Training."

"Are you two finished?" Jessie asked a moment later, somewhat sarcastically. She knew her friends were just trying to be helpful, but their enthusiasm was actually painful.

"First of all," Jessie got right to the heart of the matter, "my father is never going to let me take four days off from school. He's freaked out as it is because my grades in math aren't good enough. Then, on top of that, there'd be no one to do the work at home. He doesn't have anyone to help him," she declared, raising her arms in a helpless gesture of finality.

"Jess!" Dara wailed, and then got up and raced over to where her friend was sitting. She put her hands on her shoulders and shook her gently. "You've just got to go. We won't go without you."

"Yeah," Kate bellowed. "We'll find a way to get around your father."

Dara sat down next to Jessie, who was not the least bit encouraged by her friends' optimism. They didn't know her father like she did.

"Look ..." She decided to make one more attempt at convincing them of the gloomy reality of the situation. "My dad hurt his back pretty bad, so he was out of work for a while, and right now we don't have a housekeeper. Do you really think he's going to let me run around the state to three-day events? There'd be no one to do the chores.'"

The serious expression on Kate's face suggested that she was beginning to get new insight into Jessie's predicament.

"That's it. I just can't go!" The bitter truth hung in the air like a heavy dark cloud, raining sadness on all of them.

"I can't believe it," Dara sighed. "I thought we were all going together."

"It won't be the same without you, Jess," Kate added.

"Aw, cut it out," Jessie ordered. "It isn't so bad." She cleared her throat, and shook her head in an effort to jar herself out of an oncoming depression.

Jessie knew it would take her best acting performance to convince Kate and Dara that she really didn't care about not being able to go, but there was no way she was going to let her situation get them down or dampen their enthusiasm. If she tried hard enough, she could hide the part of her, deep inside, that felt totally defeated by her personal problems and wanted to get as far-away from everything and everybody as she possibly could. Since she didn't seem to have any control over her life anymore, *and* since her father had quit listening to her entirely, *and* since she had no hope of getting anywhere with Time-Out if she couldn't get the time to work her or show her, she might as well quit! Quit school, quit riding ... quit everything!

Kate turned to Dara with an expression of both surprise and concern when Jessie, after a moment's pause, attempted to conclude the conversation by saying, "After all, I really don't care that much about Windsor, since I'll probably be gone by then. ..."

Chapter 7

JESSIE had been as surprised as her friends were on the night of Kate's pajama party, when she had informed them that she might be gone during the Windsor Trials. It had been an outburst that had come from somewhere within, independent of her conscious thinking. After she said it, though, Jessie realized that she desperately needed some time away from her day-to-day situation so she could try to regain some perspective and relax enough to find a way to cope with her ongoing problems.

"What do you mean?" Kate had asked her, wide-eyed with curiosity and concern.

"Oh, I've just been thinking of visiting Lynne in Massachusetts, to get away for a while," Jessie had answered, and her unexpected announcement that she was going away had truly alarmed Kate and Dara.

Now Jessie was acting on her decision, even sooner than she had expected. It was the following Friday afternoon, and she haphazardly stuffed a few clothes into her backpack, feeling as if she were racing against time. Over the past few days the idea of actually leaving Smithfield—even for a little while—became more and more appealing. Finally, the need for space, time, and the understanding she knew she would get from her friend Lynne took a firm hold on her and she decided to run away.

I'm not really *running away*, Jessie thought as she emerged from the bathroom, toothbrush in hand. After all, she was only actually planning to be away for the weekend. But a sense of delinquency gripped her heart at knowing she could never tell her father her plan because, very simply, he would not let her go. In fact, she and her father had arrived at an all-time low in their communications. He was so uptight and ill-tempered lately from working with a bad back, and was turning into such a staunch disciplinarian that she didn't even dare leave a note telling him where she was going. He would probably jump in the car and come after her.

Jessie checked her purse for the money she had taken out of her savings account that afternoon, and then panicked when she looked at the clock and realized she had only twenty-five minutes to get to the station in order to make the five o'clock bus. That would put her in Ogden at about nine, when Lynne had agreed to meet her.

Jessie ran down the stairs and through the kitchen, grabbing an apple and a banana on her way out. Tonight she would miss dinner.

In what seemed like no time, she was sitting

aboard a Greyhound bus bound for Ogden, Massachusetts. It would be an understatement to say she was uncomfortable, thinking back over her day and trying to make sure she had taken care of everything. She had actually confided in Dennis, the most trustworthy of the grooms, so she could be sure he would feed and groom Time-Out. She also left a note for Anne, explaining that she wouldn't be able to work that weekend, and then had simply walked away, without telling Kate or Dara because she knew they would have tried to stop her. Despite an overwhelming feeling of frenzy, Jessie sighed and sank back into her seat, knowing that in responding to the quiet inner voice that had told her to go, she was acting in her best interest.

Jessie fell asleep during the last half of the long trip, probably in an effort to drown out her anxiety. When she woke, the sun had set and it was dark, and she was just moments away from Ogden. She barely had time to shake herself awake and get her bearings when the bus pulled up to the stop.

"Jessie!" She heard Lynne's familiar voice the moment she stepped off the bus. Lynne dashed forward to meet her friend and greeted her with a big hug. Jessie could see Mr. Stevens in the distance, leaning up against his red truck.

"I'm so glad you came," Lynne said, and grabbed Jessie's backpack with one hand and her arm with another. She hurried her along across the platform. "Come on. Let's get out of here. I want to get home so we can talk."

"Okay." Jessie shivered, feeling as if she were still asleep.

"Good to see you again, Jessie." Mr. Stevens spoke first after they had started on their way.

Before Jessie could respond, Lynne interrupted. "I'm so excited you're here. I've got lots of things planned for us to do."

"That's great," Jessie said weakly. She still wasn't quite sure where she was, and just exactly how she had gotten there.

As they drove into the Stevenses' driveway, Jessie could see Lynne's mother standing in the doorway waiting to greet them. She gave Jessie a warm welcome hug. The sweet smell of recently baked cookies filled the room, and as soon as she took off her jacket, Jessie sat down to dig in to the dinner that had been kept warm for her.

Mrs. Stevens poured a large glass of milk and set it on the table, and then pushed up the sleeves of her soft yellow sweater.

"Weren't you going to go out and feed Buster?" she asked Lynne. Buster was the family mascot, an old Irish setter who lived in his own doghouse next to the garage.

"Oh, yeah, I forgot," Lynne replied. She jumped up from the table and grabbed a down jacket from off a hook next to the doorway. "I'll be back in a second, Jessie." She smiled. "Then we can go upstairs and catch up."

After the loud thump of the screen door closing, the kitchen became oddly quiet. Jessie scraped up the last bit of potato on her plate with the side of her fork, and then pushed it away from her. Eyes cast downward, she gathered up the dark blue cotton napkin from her lap and gently laid it on the table. Sure enough, when she looked up, Mrs. Stevens was watching her.

"You know, Lynne was so excited when she heard you were coming. She's awfully fond of you," Mrs. Stevens said.

"I like her, too, ma'am," Jessie replied softly.

"Oh, Jessie. Please call me Louise," Mrs. Stevens said. She pulled out a chair and sat down.

In an attempt to avoid Louise's eyes, Jessie looked down at her hands. Evidence of Time-Out was ever present in the bits of saddle soap and grease permanently embedded under her short nails.

"You know, dear," Louise inevitably began, "when Lynne told me you were going to visit, I was a little bit surprised, knowing what your life is like at home. I didn't think you would be able to get away at this time of year." She paused a moment before going on, as if giving Jessie a chance to offer some kind of explanation.

Jessie's cheeks suddenly felt hot. She squirmed in her chair and began to jab nervously at the leg of the table with the toe of her tennis shoe.

"I wonder if you want to tell me about it," Louise said softly, leaning toward Jessie with a gentle smile.

"What's to tell?" Jessie's initial response was defensive. She was getting so tired of the whole mess, all she wanted to do was forget it. But problems never got solved by ignoring them, and Jessie knew that sooner or later she would have to talk about it.

"My father doesn't know I'm here," Jessie blurted

out. "I knew he wouldn't let me come if I told him." At the thought of her father, Jessie began to cry softly. The truth was, she already missed him.

"Oh, Jessie," Mrs. Stevens's voice was filled with sympathy and understanding. "Don't feel so bad. We know you would never purposely hurt anyone. I'm sure if you felt you needed to take a break from all your work, it really was important, and that you did the right thing."

Louise's soothing, supportive words allowed Jessie to drop her heavy head and indulge in a good, hard cry. Her entire body heaved as she sobbed, searching for release from the pent-up anxieties that had been constricting her. Lynne's mother reached out and held on to Jessie, and simply let her empty herself of all her tears before speaking.

"You know, Jessie," she gently suggested when, with a deep sigh, Jessie's crying subsided to a series of quiet whimpers, "you can call your father and tell him you're here."

Jessie reached up unconsciously and pulled her hair into a ponytail at the back of her neck, twisted it into a small knot, and then released it, so that her silky brown tresses again fell back and framed her face. "Yes, I guess I could call him," she replied weakly.

"It doesn't mean you'd have to go home," Louise added, "but I think it would make you feel better. And I know he must be wondering where you are."

What Louise was saying made sense, and suddenly Jessie felt as if she couldn't wait to talk to him.

"Thank God," he cried when he heard her voice. "You're safe."

"I'm sorry, Dad." Jessie felt a little ashamed. "I didn't mean to make you worry."

"Where are you?" he wanted to know. He seemed so far away.

"I'm in Ogden with my friend Lynne. I'm okay," Jessie said simply.

"Why did you run away?" Mr. Robeson asked.

"I don't know," Jessie told him. "I just had to get away for a while, and I didn't think you would—"

"It's okay," her father interrupted her. "I think I know why you did it. I don't mind your being there with the Stevenses," he said more calmly, as if he might have regained his equilibrium. "But it might be wise to think twice before you miss any more school."

"I know, Dad," Jessie assured him. "I'll probably come back Sunday night." Even though she felt immensely relieved to have called him, she knew they were still far from any real reconciliation. It would take even greater courage to go home and face him, and to sit down and begin the real work on their problems.

"Let me talk with Mrs. Stevens before you hang up," Jessie's father requested. Like it or not, she was still only sixteen. "I hope you know I miss you." His voice became thick with emotion. "And I love you, Jessie."

Jessie's heart leapt at the sound of his words. She had needed to hear it so badly. "Me, too, Daddy," she reassured him, and handed the phone to Mrs. Stevens.

Just at that moment Lynne burst back into the
kitchen. She's probably been standing outside,
waiting until we finished, Jessie thought.

"What took you so long?" Jessie asked. The
conversation with her father had definitely reen-
ergized her.

"Buster couldn't find his bone." Lynne hung up
her jacket and turned to her guest. "Come on.
Let's get out of this dumb kitchen."

The two friends ran up the stairs to Lynne's
room. Lynne had grabbed the plate of cookies as
she passed the table, and they now sat sprawled
out on the circular rug under her window, munching noisily. "Maybe you can help me at Featherstone
tomorrow so we can get done early and take the
afternoon off."

"I'd be glad to," Jessie said. Once the crisis
with her father was over, it didn't take Jessie long
to figure out that she had the chance for a stu-
pendous weekend. Also, working with Lynne at
Featherstone would give her the perfect opportunity to see Ed.

"I don't suppose you're interested in the fact
that my next-door neighbor has been constantly
asking about you." Lynne seemed to be able to
read her thoughts.

"Oh, really." Jessie tried to act nonchalant. She
wondered if she should tell Lynne about Ed's
letter.

Lynne sat up to untie her sneaker, and then
with sudden jerk, she kicked it high in the air so
it landed across the room.

"Like every time he sees me, he asks if I've
heard from you." Lynne snickered. "At first I didn't

mind, but now he's starting to be a real pain in the neck." She got rid of her other sneaker in a similar fashion. "Funny thing what love can do to a man."

Jessie responded with a nervous giggle. The thought of seeing Ed made her feel scared and shy. How was she ever going to face him?

"In this case, one Jessica Robeson has managed to reduce a perfectly normal guy into a simpering jellyfish," Lynne declared.

"I have not," Jessie insisted. Now she was embarrassed.

"You'll see tomorrow. He really likes you." Lynne's expression was faintly devious.

"Lynne!" Jessie sat up. "If you do or say anything weird tomorrow, you're going to get it."

"Don't be silly." Lynne laughed at her friend's dramatics. "You must think I'm a real jerk. Honest, Jess, I promise I won't say anything."

Jessie and Lynne went on to talk about their horses, and Jessie was reminded again of her problems. In leaving so abruptly, she hadn't said good-bye to Time-Out, and now she felt as if she had deserted her.

"Don't worry," Lynne tried to reassure her just before they turned out the light to go to sleep. "You got a good groom to take care of her, didn't you?"

"Yeah." Jessie knew Dennis would keep her well-fed and watered. "But I forgot to tell her I was going away. I wonder if she misses me."

"If you don't stop worrying and start to relax some, I'm going to ship you back where you came from," Lynne said, and laughed.

Jessie responded with a smile.

"Now listen. You're here for a vacation, to get away from it all. Tomorrow after we're done with the stalls and you get a chance to see Romeo, you can come with me to a little competition I entered. Mom's cooking will take care of what ails you. And if you don't feel like going home, you can stay all next week...."

"Can't," Jessie reminded her. "I have to go back for school."

"We'll see," Lynne quipped. "Doctor's orders."

Jessie sank back against her pillow and pulled the warm down quilt up to her chin. Everything has turned out okay after all, she thought. For the next couple of days she could relax and forget about work, forget about school, and let herself have a real vacation. When she got back, she would talk to her father and maybe they could straighten things out.

Jessie fell asleep pleased with her decision to come to Ogden and only slightly distressed by the nagging regret that she had forgotten to tell Time-Out good-bye.

Chapter 8

"GIRLS, don't eat so fast," said Mrs. Stevens. She was standing at the stove, spatula in hand, flipping flapjacks for her hungry family.

"I'll have a couple more, Ma," Mr. Stevens drawled, and lapped up the last bite on his plate after swishing it through the syrup.

"Mmm, these are good," Jessie exclaimed. "Real maple syrup."

"We get it from our own property," Mr. Stevens remarked proudly. "Come back in the spring and we'll show you how it's done. Even put you to work."

"Don't forget to take your vitamin." Mrs. Stevens cut her husband short. They had more than enough to do that day without worrying about next spring.

"Gee, it's gonna be after seven when we get there," Lynne complained. She jumped up from the table. "Hurry up, Jessie. If we don't get over to

Featherstone and start work soon, we'll be late for the horse show."

The two girls grabbed light windbreakers and ran out the door in the direction of Featherstone Farm.

"Don't slam the screen..." Jessie heard Louise's cry and then the *bang!* of the door.

It was early Saturday morning, and Lynne's usual routine was to go to Featherstone and work for several hours cleaning stalls. Afterward she exercised the horses. Most of the horses were still out in the paddock, and her job was to bring them in for their seven A.M. feeding after mucking out and cleaning the buckets. Today, since Jessie was there, Lynne had informed the owners that she was going to dispense with her afternoon chores.

"Grab a pitchfork," Lynne said to Jessie when they reached the barn. "Altogether we've got eleven stalls to do, so we'd better get going. I'll measure the feed and fill the hay nets, and we can both water when that's done."

Jessie grabbed a fork and began mucking out the stall that was last in line. It wasn't her favorite job, by any means, and sometimes in the stifling heat of summer it could feel near-fatal. But on the other hand, she really didn't begrudge the fact that she had to clean up after the horses. The pleasure they gave her in return made it well worth it.

Jessie poked a strand of loose hair up and over an ear, and stopped for a moment to rest. She was aware that Ed might pop in at any time, and her eyes kept darting toward the door. As a matter of fact, she had just gotten to Prince Hal's stall, and Jessie caught herself giving it an extra good cleaning. "Might as well make him comfortable," she muttered.

"Hey, Jessie," Lynne called from the stall across the aisle. "You don't have to get rid of every little piece of hay." Jessie was slightly embarrassed that Lynne had noticed how much time she was spending on Ed's horse.

When the stalls were clean and the barn swept, Lynne and Jessie went out to fetch the horses and bring them in. This was one of Jessie's favorite jobs. She loved calling the horses, and was always amazed that they responded to their names.

"Here, Crystal." Jessie held up the rope to show to the year-old filly who pranced toward her from across the field. Jessie could immediately see that this youngster was full of vinegar, and that she probably spent a good deal of time cavorting around the fields. Jessie reached up to pick a piece of grass out of her dark mane, which was decorated with strands of hay. Her bushy tail was entwined with a stick that was beating out her every step.

"My, but you're messy," Jessie admonished Crystal as she fit her halter. In return the playful young horse nudged her on the shoulder, as if to say, "A horse my age doesn't have to look good. I just want to have fun." Still, she stood quietly while Jessie removed the stick from her tail.

"Hey, Jessie!" someone called out just as she was locking the bottom latch on Crystal's stall.

Jessie looked up and saw Ed walking toward her. "Hi," she called back. Unable to conceal her pleasure, she flashed him a dazzling smile.

"Lynne said you might be coming back for a visit," he smiled back, and then stood leaning against a cross beam. In a low voice, intended only for Jessie, he asked, "Did you get my letter?"

"Yes, I did, thanks," Jessie replied shyly. "I meant to answer, but . . ."

"It's okay. I'd rather have you here in person any day." Ed didn't seem to have any trouble expressing his feelings.

Just then Lynne appeared, leading a pregnant mare into the adjoining stall. After removing her halter and making sure she had both locks on the stall door securely fastened, Lynne walked over to join Ed and Jessie.

"Hi, there, Romeo . . . I mean Ed," Lynne teased. Rather than being mad, Jessie gave her a quick look of warning and then broke out into a fit of laughter.

Ed seemed to be used to the fact that girls often got the giggles, and he simply stood there quietly, waiting for them to subside.

"What are you going to do today?" he asked Lynne.

"We're trying to finish up here and then we're going over to Barnsville for the local horse show."

"Local is right," Ed said flatly. "Are you in it?"

"Yes, I am." Lynne seemed slightly insulted. "Local or not, I see it as a chance to practice."

"I *want* to go," Jessie defended Lynne. "Besides, you always learn something from these things."

Ed immediately acquiesced. "You're right," he said, and, turning to Jessie, "Mind if I tag along? We can root for Lynne from the sidelines."

"Sure," Jessie exclaimed, suddenly aware of her fluttering heart. Somehow she kept her cool long enough to make specific plans to meet Ed at the competition.

"Poor guy," Lynne later remarked to Jessie as they strolled back to the farm. She was leading Dolly, and Jessie was leading a horse named Jazz. "He's really got it bad for you."

"What do you mean?" Jessie wasn't sure she understood her.

"Ah, come on," Lynne implored. "You know what I mean. Didn't you see the way he was looking at you?"

"How? How was he looking at me?" Jessie demanded. She stopped walking her horse and turned around on the single lane path to face Lynne.

"Don't be such a nerd," Lynne insisted. "The guy obviously has a super colossal crush on you. And don't tell me you didn't notice."

"Well, I did catch him staring at me once or twice," Jessie said. "But I'd rather ride horses any day than sit around talking with a guy. So far, they're only good for dancing." Jessie intentionally played down her interest in Ed so Lynne wouldn't feel like a third wheel. She knew what that was like from being with Dara when she started going on about Doug.

After a midmorning snack of yogurt and fruit back at the house, Jessie and Lynne saddled their horses for a short ride. Jessie held up an apple in the flat palm of her hand and offered it to her horse, Jazz. Jazz was a fine deep brown brood mare with long, sloping shoulders and prominent withers. Lynne had told Jessie that Jazz had foaled earlier in the year and that her enormous, leggy colt had permanently damaged her uterus during the birthing process. Since she was too old to be returned to competition, she would have to be sold as a family pet, and could be lightly hacked. "We'll just have to hope we find some good folks to buy her who really love her," Lynne concluded.

Jessie felt Jazz's good vibrations before she even mounted her, and knew at once she was special. I'm not going to have any trouble with you, Jessie acknowledged, sensing that Jazz was a truly good-natured animal.

Mr. Stevens had converted a grassy area behind the garage into a dressage ring of sorts, and Lynne asked Jessie to watch her and Dolly go through a few quick paces.

"I want to see what you think," Lynn said as she and Dolly approached the ring to begin. "We've been practicing pretty hard, and I think we're finally getting somewhere."

Lynne and Dolly warmed up quickly and then went through parts of the test, exhibiting a free walk and then a collected walk. At Lynne's command, Dolly moved into a powerful collected trot, followed by a breathtaking extension. Then a medium trot and finally into a graceful canter. All of the transitions looked supple and correct, and Jessie could sense the harmonious relationship between horse and rider that was reflected in the ease and lightness with which Dolly responded. They were clearly ready to perform.

"Bravo," Jessie shouted, and nudged Jazz into motion. They walked over to the center line where Lynne and Dolly were standing. "That was excellent," she told Lynne sincerely. "You look so much better than you did at the Ogden trials. You must have been practicing night and day."

"Well, we've been working pretty hard, I have to admit," Lynne said, and patted her horse on the neck. "I'd really like to enter Windsor."

Jessie actually jumped when she heard Lynne mention Windsor, the source of so much of her worry. She successfully managed to change the subject by asking about the competition they were going to attend that day. They could discuss Windsor later.

As it turned out, Jessie was right about Lynne and Dolly's hard work paying off. Local or not, they were the stars of the Barnsville show.

Since it was so close, Lynne rode Dolly over to the Peet Farm where the Barnsville competition was being held. Jessie went in the car with Mrs. Stevens, and when they got there, she was relieved to see Ed already waiting for her.

"Hey, Jessie, over here." He waved.

Mrs. Stevens nodded her permission for Jessie to join him. It was hard for Jessie not to feel self-conscious as she approached Ed, since she knew he was watching her the entire way.

"How do they look?" Jessie asked quickly, referring to the other riders.

"They look young. And green," Ed said frankly.

Jessie was surprised when she saw that many of the kids competing were probably no more than twelve or thirteen years old. A small group looked as if they were Lynne's age. She remembered that she was very young when she had started riding, so she certainly couldn't knock them—or their amateur performances.

"Want to sit down?" Ed asked, pointing to a couple of rows of folding chairs that had been set up outside the ring.

"Sure." Jessie tried to sound casual, but felt a nervous shiver when Ed took her elbow and led her over to a chair.

During the competition, it seemed as if the young riders' biggest job was to simply keep their horses attentive and, if they were lucky, somewhat relaxed. Jessie found herself laughing along with Ed when one horse got so interested in a patch of clover that was growing alongside the fence in the warm-up area that he absolutely wouldn't budge, and refused to go into the ring.

"I like to come to these because you get to see all the things that *could* go wrong if a horse isn't trained right," Jessie explained to Ed, who nodded his agreement.

"That horse is never going to do anything if the rider doesn't relax," Ed said as a young girl and her dappled gray circled the ring.

"Look at how she's perching. I bet she never sat back and drove a horse forward," Jessie commented.

"Pretty basic stuff, I'd say."

"But not as easy as it looks."

As they sat, side by side, giving the performers their "professional" critiques, Jessie began to relax and have fun. Delicate clouds whisked across the deep blue afternoon sky, and a gentle breeze ruffled the ends of her hair. Gee, she thought as she stole a quick glance at Ed, it's nice being with a guy who knows so much about horses. Maybe we're really going to get along.

"Hey, look." Ed sat up and pointed across the ring. "Here comes Lynne. Looks like she's ready for dressage."

"Lynne told me the director from the Dressage Federation is here," Jessie informed Ed.

"Here! In Barnsville?" He couldn't believe it. "Well," he concluded after Lynne and Dolly had entered the ring in perfect form and saluted the judge, "he'll see at least one great performance."

"Yeah," Jessie agreed. "I watched Lynne and Dolly this morning, and they were polished."

"You aren't kidding. That was a beautiful half circle. And look at how smooth they are going into that trot."

Jessie was just as impressed as Ed, and happy for her friend.

Lynne and Dolly's final turn down the center line was perfect, and it clinched them the blue ribbon.

"I'm glad to hear they're entering Windsor. They're going to do great in Novice," Ed said after it was over.

"Yes," Jessie replied weakly. She had better reconcile herself to the fact that Kate and Dara weren't the only ones thinking about Windsor. Both Lynne and Ed were probably going, too.

Jessie stood up and stretched, and Ed got to his feet and looked over at her.

"You wouldn't be up for walking back, would you?" he asked. "We can cut across the fields, so it's only a little over a mile."

"Okay," Jessie answered shyly. She turned and followed him through the crowd of people who were mingling around the winners. After congratulating Lynne and informing Mrs. Stevens that she was going back with Ed, Jessie found herself walking alongside him, heading across the fields in the direction of the farm.

"How did you like the competition?" Ed asked.

"Oh, it was fun. Nothing too spectacular, except for Lynne. But Anne, my trainer, says we should go to things like this so we can develop observation skills. It'll help us with our riding."

Ed simply looked at her and smiled. They walked on for a while in silence, until a few moments later Jessie felt Ed's fingers graze her palm, and before she knew it, they were holding hands.

At first Jessie didn't really feel comfortable holding Ed's hand, but soon they fell into a natural rhythm, and a new feeling of warmth surged through her. When Ed broke the ice and began telling her more about Featherstone Farm, she actually began to relax.

"I worked Prince Hal a little this morning. He just gets better and better," Ed began. "Then I helped the maintenance crew mend some fence over on the far paddock. I kind of like to learn how to do everything."

Jessie nodded in agreement. She was glad that Ed wasn't afraid of manual labor, and that as the owner's son, he didn't feel he was above it all.

After wending their way through a wedge of poplars that separated the fields, Jessie saw they were already back on the Stevenses' property, at the edge of the far field.

"Would you like to go riding with me again tomorrow morning, Jessie?" Ed asked as they approached the house.

"Sure." Jessie smiled up at him. They stood facing each other just outside the Stevenses' back door. Suddenly an outrageous idea raced through Jessie's mind and made her stomach lurch. He's going to kiss me, she thought, not knowing exactly what to do.

Instead, Ed simply put his hand up to her cheek for a brief moment, and Jessie was instantly relieved. Neither of them was ready.

"See you tomorrow," Ed said softly, and slowly walked off toward home. When he turned to look back at her, Jessie waved him on, and then waltzed inside on air. Her day with Ed had been perfect!

"You look like the cat who swallowed the canary," Lynne said when she saw Jessie come in. She was heading toward the dinner table carrying a plate of crispy baked chicken.

"Lynne," Jessie warned her, not wanting her mother to hear. But it was impossible to keep her quiet once she started laughing.

"What did he do, kiss you?" Lynne whispered to Jessie as she swished past her to retrieve the salad from the refrigerator and bring it to the table.

"No!" Jessie insisted, "and if you say one more word ..."

Jessie could have died of embarrassment when Mr. and Mrs. Stevens walked into the dining room just after she had taken a friendly swipe at their daughter.

"I wonder if it would be possible for us to eat now?" Lynne's mother smiled over at Lynne's father, obviously amused by the girls' horseplay.

Jessie thought she had never been so hungry, and hurriedly gobbled up the delicious meal as if it were her last. After everyone had finished, she remembered her manners, and offered to do the dishes.

"That's very nice of you," Mrs. Stevens said graciously. "We'll just go into the living room and put up our feet."

After dinner, Lynne didn't seem to be her usual talkative self, and Jessie could see that she was tired from the competition. It took some convincing, but finally Lynne went into the living room to watch TV. Jessie would take care of the dishes.

While she was filling up the porcelain sink with bubbling hot water, Jessie was distracted from her job by thoughts of Windcroft and Time-Out. She wondered if it would be too late to call Kate after dinner, to find out how everyone was doing.

"I really miss you," she mumbled to her absentee friends as she scrubbed at the bottom of a glass baking dish. Jessie began to fantasize about how much fun it would be if Kate and Dara were with her. The thought made her feel uneasy, and lonely for her friends, her family, and for Time-Out.

She tried to shake the nervous feeling in the pit

of her stomach as she carefully dried and put away the dishes. Jessie couldn't remember when she had felt so odd. I hope this state of mind is from all the excitement of being in Ogden, she thought, and isn't some kind of weird premonition.

After Jessie had finished up the dishes, she reached up and turned out the overhead light. As she stood alone in the dark kitchen, she couldn't help but wonder again, could there really be something wrong? A cold chill shot up her spine.

Chapter 9

As it turned out, Jessie's uneasy feelings about Windcroft remained with her the entire evening. After doing the dishes, she rejoined Lynne and her parents in their Early American–style living room with flocked wallpaper and antique furniture, and they all played Scrabble for the next hour or so. By the time Jessie remembered she had wanted to call Kate, it was nearly ten P.M., too late for phone calls at a working horse farm.

Even though Scrabble wasn't one of Jessie's favorite games, she did enjoy the lighthearted competition between the Stevenses, who were all really trying to win. Jessie was told that neither of the women had ever been able to consistently beat Mr. Stevens, a crossword puzzle enthusiast. Sure enough, he won again, but was neck and neck with Lynne, until, at the very end, he found a word that used up all his letters.

"Good game, girls." Mr. Stevens gloated a little, but it was all in fun. He put his arm around his daughter's shoulders and gave her a friendly hug. "A little more practice and maybe you'll be as good as your pa." He smiled.

Jessie, Lynne, and Louise all vowed they would get him the next game. Then, noticing the clock, Louise informed the girls it was time for them to go to bed.

"You've got another long day tomorrow, and I'm sure you must be pooped. Especially you, Jessie." She had noticed that Jessie was fidgety and nervous all through their game. "Are you feeling okay?" she asked.

"Oh, yeah," Jessie responded. "Guess I'm just a little tired." Jessie wasn't about to tell them she had a premonition about home, and was worried that something was wrong there. Between running away and now her ridiculous case of clairvoyance, they would think she was absolutely mad!

Just before they went upstairs, Jessie had an opportunity to speak with Louise for a moment alone.

"Would it be all right with you if I went riding with Ed in the morning?" she asked. They were standing in the kitchen, where Louise was checking the table to make sure everything was put away.

"You did a nice job here, Jessie," she said, sponging off a few last crumbs from the counter. "Yes, I think it would be fine if you and Ed went riding. He's such a nice boy; I don't have any objections, and I'm sure your father wouldn't mind."

"Oh, thanks," Jessie gushed. She rushed up to

Louise and kissed her on the cheek. "Thanks for everything," she added. "You've made me feel so much at home."

"Well, we want you to know you're always welcome here," Louise said, pleased with Jessie's good manners—as well as her spontaneous display of affection.

"You're lucky to have such a nice mom and dad," Jessie told Lynne later on, when they were upstairs in her room.

"They're all right, I guess," Lynne said. "I'm sure your father's pretty cool, too, when he isn't working so hard."

"Yeah, he is," Jessie confirmed.

But Lynne didn't want to talk about her parents. "Come on. Out with it. What happened with Ed?" There was no way Jessie was going to get off without telling her.

"Oh, we just talked." She tried to sound casual. "And he asked me to go riding with him again in the morning." She paused. Now came the tough part. "I know how much you hate getting up early on Sunday, so I'll just set the alarm and get dressed quietly. . . ."

"Are you trying to tell me you don't want me to go with you?" Lynne tried to feign disappointment, but she wound up laughing instead. "You're not going to actually try and convince me that you and Ed had any intention of asking me. Besides . . ."—she studied her nails nonchalantly as she spoke—"it would probably make me sick, watching you two lovebirds make goo-goo eyes at each other all morning. No, thank you," she concluded. "I'm perfectly happy to stay in bed."

Jessie smiled at her friend. She was really having such fun being there. But still, the feeling of dread that had settled in the pit of her stomach was still there, and she decided to mention it to Lynne.

"Did you ever have anything like a premonition?" Jessie began. "You know, did you ever think you could tell what was happening in some other place?" She tried not to sound too silly.

"Oh, you mean like ESP?" Lynne asked her instantly, as if she were familiar with the subject.

"I don't know if you'd call it that. . . ."

"Well . . ."—Lynne launched into a story—"one time in the winter after a big snowfall my dad's car went off the road and he got knocked out. My mom and I were at home, waiting for him, but, you know, we really didn't know why he was late or what had happened." Lynne leaned toward Jessie and continued dramatically, "Suddenly my mother jumped up. It was really weird. She insisted that we get in the truck and go looking for him—in all that snow. She drove straight to the place where it had happened, and we saved him."

"Wow!" Jessie was impressed.

"I still don't know how she knew he was there. She just said she got this feeling that kind of took over her, and that she could sense exactly where he was."

"Too much," Jessie exclaimed. "Maybe it's 'cause they're married, and they're so close, they can feel where the other person is."

"Yeah," Lynne affirmed the possibility.

"You know," Jessie spoke again after a moment, "I've been feeling kind of funny when I think about Windcroft, and especially about my horse."

"What do you mean?" Lynne asked, interested.

"Well, it's just kind of like a scared feeling here, in my stomach." She patted her abdomen as she spoke. "I can't help but wonder if everything is all right. You don't think anything could be wrong, do you?" she asked Lynne earnestly.

Lynne was silent for a moment. A momentary look of fear flashed in her eyes, as if she were imagining some tragedy at Windcroft, just to test the reality of Jessie's "premonition." But she seemed to quickly reject the notion. "No. There wouldn't be anything wrong at Windcroft. You've got all those people there looking after the place. I'm sure Time-Out's feeling as fit and sassy as ever. She probably doesn't even miss you." Lynne was trying to make Jessie feel better, but her last remark didn't help.

"Well, I miss her a lot," Jessie stated, "and I know she *must* miss me. Especially since I forgot to say good-bye." She knew she probably sounded dumb, but then Lynne did understand how close she was to Time-Out.

"I didn't mean she probably doesn't know you're gone," Lynne corrected herself. "But I'm sure she's not moping around, thinking you're never coming home."

"I guess you're right." Jessie sighed as she got into bed and snuggled in for the night. Still, she wasn't entirely convinced.

Lynne could sense Jessie's lingering frustration, and tried once more to appease her. "Come on, Jessie. You're just homesick. It's a feeling we all get when we go away."

"I guess so," Jessie conceded. She reached for the clock on the night table and quickly set the alarm. But I didn't feel homesick the last time I was here, Jessie thought to herself, still not convinced that her friend was right.

The two girls said good night and Lynne turned out the light. Jessie was left alone with her fears, which were not about to retire. She tossed and turned for what seemed forever and then she was dreaming. . . .

In the dream Jessie was at a horse show that was taking place in a clearing on the edge of a dense forest. The forest itself was dark and forbidding, and the huge old trees with gnarled limbs and spiky branches stood like sentries, guarding its entrance.

Jessie strained her eyes to see more clearly. It was so dark. But suddenly lightning struck, lighting the forest, and then it started to pour. Thunder roared as streaks of silver flashed across the sky. The rain fell in torrents that slammed against the earth. It was then, at the height of the storm, that Jessie heard the voice of one of the judges.

"Time-Out," he ordered. "Approach the line."

Jessie simply couldn't believe her ears when she heard him call Time-Out to the starting box to begin her cross-country test.

"No!" she protested loudly. "It's too dangerous. The event must be canceled." But no one could hear her.

Jessie was even more horrified when she saw

*Time-Out suddenly appear, ready to begin. "Wait!"
she cried. "Time-Out, stop!"*

*Nevertheless, Time-Out began the course, run-
ning in a state of terror. She took off down the
trail at a gallop, all the time fighting off the
needlelike rain that was blinding her eyes and
lashing at her back.*

*Perhaps even more frightening than the vision
of Time-Out was the recognition of her rider. Is
that me? Jessie thought frantically. Like the horse,
the girl on Time-Out's back was in a state of
panic. She looked enough like Jessie to make her
think it was her double, and again Jessie tried to
warn her. "I'm here. I'm Jessie. I don't know who
you are, but I want you to go back. That's my
horse you're riding."*

*The rider flashed a defiant look at Jessie, and
she suddenly had the eerie realization that she
was both watching her dream and at the same
time was in it. The rider hung onto Time-Out for
dear life as they stumbled along the slippery trail
that led to disaster.*

*Jessie thought she heard the faint sound of snick-
ering from the two judges who stood up ahead on
the far side of a ravine. Even though it was still
raining, they sat on their horses, score sheets in
hand, seemingly laughing.*

*"Noooo," Jessie screamed, trying in vain to break
through so that Time-Out could hear her.*

*The ravine was too wide, and the footing was
slippery; it was impossible to tell what was on the
other side. Time-Out took a frantic leap and landed
on mucky, loose shale banking—ground that gave
way immediately and pitched both horse and rider*

forward to their fatal destiny. Jessie felt herself
sliding up and over Time-Out's back and down
onto the sharp, slippery shale that pierced her
consciousness and made her awaken. . . .

"Help!" Jessie leapt up in bed, truly frightened.
Little beads of sweat laced her forehead, and her
entire body was shaking. My God, she thought,
where am I? What happened? Then she remembered the nightmare.

Jessie looked over at Lynne, who was sleeping
peacefully. Reaching up to wipe a tear from the
corner of her eye, she couldn't believe how real
the nightmare had seemed. When she was little
and had a bad dream, her mother always stayed
with her until she felt better. Now she was alone,
and she could only pray that she would quickly
shake off her terror. She drew the blanket up
around her shoulders, and hugged her arms to
her chest.

I'm never going to go back to sleep, she thought
desperately, after looking at the clock and lying
back in bed. I don't care who's still sleeping, she
decided, in two hours, at six o'clock, I'm going to
call Kate.

If she did sleep again that night, Jessie didn't
know it. Every fifteen minutes or so she glanced
at the clock, feeling as if she couldn't wait another second until morning. But it was before six
when she heard a soft tapping on the bedroom
door and jumped out of bed to answer it.

Jessie was shocked when she saw Mrs. Stevens,
barefoot and in a pink flannel nightgown, standing at the foot of the stairway and beckoning her

down. "You've got a telephone call, Jessie. It's your friend Kate."

"Oh, no," Jessie wailed, and flew down the stairs. There was absolutely no question in her mind now. Something was the matter.

"Kate! What's wrong?" she screamed into the phone.

"Jessie. Calm down," Kate began diplomatically, hearing the fear in her friend's voice. "I thought I should call you and tell you that Time-Out's sick. We think it's colic. Anne just called Dr. Rosen, so we don't know how serious it is yet. But right now it doesn't look good. . . ."

Chapter 10

"JESSIE, at least drink this," Louise implored as she handed her a glass of milk. "You can't run off without eating any breakfast. It won't help matters."

Jessie drank the milk in a few gulps. She felt as if she had never been in such a hurry. After she had received the startling phone call from Kate, she had raced upstairs to pack her things while the Stevenses phoned to see about transportation back to Smithfield.

"What's happening?" Lynne asked sleepily when the noise of Jessie's slipshod packing woke her.

"I have to go back," Jessie explained in a tight, high voice. "Time-Out is sick."

"Oh, no." Lynne could hardly believe her ears. Lynne got out of bed and grabbed for her jeans and sweatshirt, and before Jessie was finished stuffing her clothes into her leather satchel, Lynne was standing by, ready to help her.

"There's a bus that leaves from Wolverton at nine," Mr. Stevens said as he walked into the kitchen. "That's about an hour from here by car. If you take it from there, it will only be three hours to Smithfield. Looks like the fastest way."

Louise grabbed her reading glasses from the counter and said, "Here, let me look." She studied the schedule for a few moments and then agreed, "Yes. It'll be much faster taking that bus than waiting for the one from here."

"That's it, then," Mr. Stevens said with finality. "I'll take you to Wolverton, so we have to get going now. Don't worry, Jessie. You should be home by noon."

Even in the face of the crisis, Jessie didn't forget her manners. She thanked Mrs. Stevens profusely for her generous hospitality before hopping into the truck. Lynne insisted on riding along to the bus. If nothing else, she could provide moral support for her friend.

But just as she was about to get into the truck, Jessie stopped and exclaimed, "Oh, my gosh. I forgot. I was going riding with Ed at eight o'clock!"

"Don't worry, Jessie. I'll call him," Mrs. Stevens offered one last favor. "I'll tell him Time-Out's sick, and that you had to go back suddenly. I'm sure he'll understand."

"Thank you," Jessie said sincerely. Then as a second thought, "Tell him I'll let him know what happens."

They arrived in Wolverton moments before the bus pulled out, and after a frantic good-bye to Lynne and her father, Jessie found herself rolling along toward Smithfield, and to her beloved Time-Out. She tried to relax and not let her imagination get the best of her, but it was difficult to remain levelheaded, plagued as she was by dismal projections about what could happen. Jessie knew that colic was very rarely fatal, and that it had probably been caught in time, but it could also be extremely painful, and her heart sank when she thought of her Time-Out suffering.

"Over here," Jessie heard Dara's voice the second after she stepped off the bus. She slung her satchel over her shoulder and ran toward the car.

"How is she?" Jessie asked before saying hello.

Dara's expression was sober, and her voice serious. "Dr. Rosen just left. He examined her pretty thoroughly and gave her a shot for pain. He doesn't think there's any danger of a rupture, but we're supposed to try and keep her from rolling so she won't twist an intestine."

Reality hit hard when Jessie heard the prognosis. "I never should have gone away!" she cried.

"Oh, come on, Jess," Dara responded. "It wasn't your fault Time-Out got colic. Even though Kate and I weren't too happy about you going away without telling us first." Dara sounded exactly like a parent.

"I thought I told you," Jessie sniffled, "when we stayed over at Kate's." If only this car could go faster, she thought frantically.

"You said you might visit, but you didn't tell us any of the details ... like *when*," Dara reminded her. Then, realizing that now was not the time for sounding gruff, Dara went on, "Anyway, it doesn't really matter. Right now the only thing we've got to be concerned about is getting Time-Out well."

Dara pulled into the Windcroft driveway and Jessie leapt out of the car and ran toward the barn, even before the car came to a full stop. When she reached Time-Out's stall, she stood gaping at her horse, horrified by what she saw.

Time-Out was standing up, pawing at the air, and occasionally letting out an eerie groan, her expression one of extreme pain. Suddenly she began leaning on the walls of her stall and biting her sides, frantic for relief. From where Jessie stood, she could see the horse had been sweating profusely.

"The vet came a couple of hours ago," Kate informed her gently. Jessie was too stunned to realize that Kate and Anne were also there. Their faces reflected concern and fatigue.

"We've been taking turns walking her," Anne said. "We thought she might want to rest awhile, but I think maybe you should take her out again. Dr. Rosen tubed her with a dose of oil and medicine and said he'd be back this afternoon to give her another shot if necessary."

"Has she thought about eating anything?" Jessie asked weakly.

"She hasn't even sniffed her hay. Sometimes she dunks her nose in the bucket of water, but she hasn't even taken a sip," Kate said, unable to conceal her concern.

"We're not out of the woods yet, I suppose," Anne admitted, "but we're doing everything we can."

It wasn't until Jessie had heard the entire dreadful report that she approached Time-Out. She said her name softly and, recognizing her voice, Time-Out turned slowly to acknowledge her.

Jessie wept silently when she saw the shavings stuck to the dried sweat on Time-Out's side. She looked into her horse's helpless, suffering eyes.

"We've got to fight this." Jessie's voice shook, and then was drowned out by the loud thud of Time-Out kicking at the side of her stall. The horse made a sudden gesture as if she wanted to lie down and roll, and Jessie knew she had to stop her.

"No! Time-Out," Jessie said in her sternest voice. "You're not going to lie down." She quickly grabbed the lead line that had been left attached to her halter and informed her, "We're going to keep walking instead." The horse leaned on the line and groaned in protest, but followed her owner out of her stall. Anne and Kate each put a hand on either side of her rump to keep her steady. "It's the only way we can help you, Time-Out," Jessie assured her.

Time-Out made no effort to disguise her pain as Jessie led her slowly around the ring. Jessie knew that the best thing to do was to keep moving. That way whatever was blocking Time-Out's system might pass through more quickly and cause less chance of intestinal twisting, which would ultimately require costly surgery and might, in the long run. . . . The rest was just too dreadful to contemplate.

"Oh, Kate, I'm so scared," Jessie confided in her friend, who was walking beside her.

"I know, but Dr. Rosen will be back again in a couple of hours, and he'll be able to tell us more." Kate tried to reassure her friend.

Jessie was once more overcome with guilt. "I never should have gone off and left her alone."

Like Dara, Kate was absolutely insistent that she mustn't blame herself. It could only make the situation worse.

"It wasn't your fault," Kate declared. "We already figured out that Time-Out got colic from eating moldy hay. The groom didn't realize when he fed her that the flakes were moldy in the middle. Hardly your doing, I'd say."

"But I knew before I left that some of the bales were moldy. I told Anne, but I should have mentioned it to Dennis, too," Jessie insisted.

"Look ..."—Kate stopped Jessie and put her hands firmly on her shoulders—"I know I'm only a few months older than you, but I'm telling you it's not doing you any good to blame yourself for what happened. You're one of the best, most responsible horsewomen I know. It was just a freak accident that made Time-Out sick." She paused for a moment and let her words sink in.

"I'm going to eat something," Kate said. "I think if you walk her for another half hour, she might want to rest again afterward. I'll be out in a while to see how she is."

"Thanks, Kate." Jessie smiled weakly, and then turned her attention back to her horse.

After their walk, Jessie led Time-Out back to her stall. Jessie winced when she saw her full hay net and untouched bucket of water. Still, Time-

Out seemed to be in less pain now, and for the next half hour she was quiet, as if on a short hiatus from her suffering.

"Hello, Jessie," Dr. Rosen said softly as he approached the stall. Jessie was relieved that Anne was with him.

"How are we doing here?" Dr. Rosen inquired of Time-Out, who had gotten to her feet when she saw the doctor, almost as if she recognized him.

"Still sweating, I see," he said. He touched a swollen spot on Time-Out's side, and the horse whinnied loudly in pain.

"She's not going to like this, but I'm going to have to give her a rectal exam," the doctor told Jessie. "It's too bad horses can't tell us, like people can, how much and where they hurt. The only way to see if she's still blocked is to examine her. You'll have to help me hold her."

Jessie felt as uncomfortable as Time-Out during the doctor's examination, and was relieved when he followed it with another shot for pain and some more medicine. "She should be okay for a while, but the shot will wear off in about two hours," the doctor informed them. Anne moved to Jessie's side and put her arm around her. "Then you can start walking her again, if she's up to it. I've got an emergency way over on the other side of the county. I'll be back in the late afternoon, say around five o'clock. We can only hope she's feeling better by then, and that the obstruction is starting to loosen up. If not,"—Dr. Rosen took off his glasses and looked directly into Jessie's eyes— "then we might be in trouble."

"She's going to get better." Anne tried to encourage Jessie, who winced in terror as her eyes watered and tears streamed down her cheeks.

"Sure, she is. These things often take time," Dr. Rosen affirmed, realizing that perhaps he had been too candid with such a young girl. Still, his policy had always been to hide nothing, and like it or not, to face up to the truth.

"Now you take good care of her, and I'll be back as soon as I can," the doctor promised as he stepped back out of the stall and walked toward the door.

The shot Dr. Rosen had administered seemed to take effect by the time he left, and Time-Out once again appeared to be resting quietly. Jessie reached down and hugged her around her neck, feeling as if she dared to make physical contact for the first time.

"Do you want to go in and lie down for a while?" Anne asked her. "I bet you could use something to eat. Or a cold drink."

"No, I don't think so," Jessie answered quickly. The last thing in the world she wanted to do was to leave Time-Out. "I can get a drink from the hose if I'm thirsty."

Jessie rested her head on top of her folded arms and leaned forward into Time-Out's stall. Once again she had the eerie sensation that she was dazed, as if in a dream. Anne stood apart from the stall and simply stared at Jessie, pondering for a moment whether or not to speak with her.

"I called your father," she finally said. "He knows you're here."

"Thanks, Anne," Jessie replied numbly.

"Jessie, Kate tells me you think this is some-how your fault, and that your going away might have contributed to Time-Out's illness," Anne be-gan. She rubbed her hand across her forehead to shove aside a lock of auburn hair that had fallen into her eyes. The stained and wrinkled flannel shirt she had on looked as if she had been wear-ing it for hours. Probably at least since early that morning, when Time-Out first got sick.

"You know, Jessie, I was the one who forgot to warn all of the grooms to look out for moldy hay. I just assumed the new batch would be okay. If you remember correctly, as soon as you noticed the mold, you told me. So if anyone is to blame for this thing, it's me. I'm so sorry. It shouldn't have slipped my mind."

"It's nobody's fault, really," Jessie said maturely, and managed to give Anne a smile. "You're the one who needs to go inside and rest for a while," she added, reversing their roles. "I really don't want to leave her now. Not even for a minute."

Anne nodded her understanding, and left Jessie and Time-Out alone. Even though she wasn't sleep-ing, Time-Out was still fairly quiet, and Jessie hoped against hope that it wasn't simply the ef-fect of the drug, but rather that the horse was getting better.

But Time-Out's dull coat and glassy eyes re-flected a different story, and when Jessie went into the stall, she again caught sight of her ago-nized expression. Time-Out whinnied her misery when she recognized Jessie, and heartfelt tears rolled down Jessie's cheeks as she sat perched beside her, trying to convey her sympathy.

"I'm here now," she whispered softly, "and you're gonna be well in no time. You've been such a brave girl," she went on steadily, rubbing her neck, "pretty soon you're going to feel just fine."

But a new well of tears suddenly erupted from Jessie's sad eyes, and she cried out in desperation, "Please, God. You've just got to make her get better...."

Chapter 11

TIME-OUT spent the next couple of hours resting, and Jessie took advantage of the break and dozed off in an old rocker that was left in the barn. But she woke up with a jolt when Time-Out once again began pawing at the sides of her stall. The shot must have worn off, Jessie concluded instantly, and she jumped up, anxious to take a good look at Time-Out and see if she could detect any improvement in her condition.

Time-Out was still very restless, and was obviously exhausted by her pain, but when she stuck out her neck toward her water bucket Jessie was immediately hopeful. All she did was dunk her nose in the water and then turn her head away, dashing Jessie's hopes that she might be getting better.

"You're still hurting pretty bad, aren't you?" Jessie tried to comfort her. "I think the best thing for us to do is to keep walking," she concluded, and led Time-Out back outside for another long, tedious stroll.

They hadn't been walking for more than ten minutes when Kate and Anne joined them. "How is she?" Both were eager to know.

"She slept for a couple of hours," Jessie told them, "but she still hasn't touched her food or water. I guess the only thing I can do is to keep on walking her," she said, sounding nearly defeated.

"Here, Jessie," Kate said, handing her a large glass of orange juice. "I know you're probably not hungry, but at least drink this. You've got to keep up your strength."

Though not hungry, Jessie followed orders and drank her juice.

In the meantime, Anne had been taking close inspection of Time-Out. "I really think she looks somewhat better, dear," she said finally. "There's a little bit more life in those eyes than I saw a few hours ago."

"Do you really think so?" Jessie asked hopefully, praying Anne was right.

"Dara called and told me to tell you to keep your chin up," Kate told Jessie after Anne had gone back into the house and they had resumed walking. "She can't come over because of a long-standing date with Doug, but she says she's going to call in every couple of hours to see how you're doing."

Jessie was touched by her friend's concern. She smiled at Kate to show her appreciation.

"Mom's got a sixth sense when it comes to horses," Kate continued, "and if she thinks Time-

Out's turned a corner, it's probably true. Even though we can't see it yet."

"I certainly hope so," Jessie sighed. She couldn't remember when she had wished for anything more. They walked on in silence for several minutes.

"I have a lot to tell you," Jessie said, "but I'm so tired, it'll just have to wait."

"I can wait," Kate responded, able to imagine how she would feel if Spy were that sick, and if there were even the slightest chance he wouldn't make it. She certainly wouldn't be in the mood for conversation with anyone. "I'm going to go back in and help Mom for a while. If you want anything at all, just holler."

Jessie and Time-Out spent the next hour walking slowly around the practice ring until Jessie lost all sense of time and felt as if they might have been stumbling along for days. When she realized how tired her own feet were getting, she led Time-Out back and into her stall.

Once inside, she expected Time-Out to start feeling her pain. Instead, Jessie was thrilled when she saw her actually walk over to her hay and sniff a choice selection and then drop it, as if she were at least acknowledging the existence of food. Likewise with her water: even though she didn't drink any, she did stick her nose in the bucket and rinse out her dry, parched mouth. As lethargic as they were, these gestures gave Jessie new hope, and she plopped down again in the rocker, believing for the first time that day that Time-Out was going to make it.

Just then Dr. Rosen entered the barn, and Jessie smiled broadly at the faithful vet, tremendously relieved to see him.

"She's quit thrashing around so much," Jessie informed him, "and she at least sniffed at her hay a few minutes ago. We've been walking all afternoon. I think she might be getting better...." She spoke anxiously, barely able to wait for the doctor's opinion.

Dr. Rosen stepped inside the stall and listened to Time-Out's belly with a stethoscope. Then he proceeded to give the horse another examination.

"Well, Jessie, you've done a great job nursing her. It looks to me as if the obstruction has moved, and her system is actually on the mend."

"You're kidding!" Jessie squealed with delight.

"Whoa, girl." Dr. Rosen spoke to Jessie as he would to Time-Out. "I said I *think*. That doesn't mean we're totally all clear yet. I'm going to give her another shot, and I want you to walk her some more after that. My guess is she should begin eating soon. Lord knows, she must be hungry. When and if she does, give me a call pronto. It'll make me sleep easier tonight."

"Yes, sir," Jessie said, and took up her post. "Just as soon as you're through, we'll go for another walk, and I'll keep you posted."

"You might think about getting a little rest yourself," Dr. Rosen said to Jessie as he left. "You look pretty beat."

"I will," Jessie promised. "As soon as Time-Out's better."

Happily Dr. Rosen's prediction turned out to be true, and after several more turns around the backyard, Time-Out soon began munching gingerly on her hay, comfortably settled back in her stall.

"Good girl," Jessie exclaimed with glee. "Now have a little water," she said, and in friendly compliance, Time-Out drank deeply.

"Oh, Time-Out," Jessie squealed, and stood on tiptoe to give her a hug. "You're going to be okay after all."

"Did I hear you right?" someone asked from behind her. Jessie recognized the voice of her father, and weary tears sprang to her eyes. The little girl in her wanted to throw herself into his arms and fold up in the warmth of his strong embrace. But somehow Jessie's reserve and the still painful memories of all that had happened between them lately got in the way, so instead she simply turned and said, "Hi, Dad."

"Jessie." Her father repeated her name, displaying his great relief at seeing his daughter. "I'm so glad you're back. Did I hear you say that Time-Out was going to make it?"

"Yes, I think so." Jessie once again felt the thrill of being released from the awesome possibilities of defeat. "She just started eating, so that means she's probably okay."

"I'm so glad," Mr. Robeson said with an intensity that surprised Jessie. She stared at him, as if she were really seeing him for the first time. Dressed casually in a forest green cardigan sweater and worn out khakis, he looked oddly at home posed against the backdrop of the barn.

"You know," he went on softly, "it's long past dinner. I was worried you hadn't eaten all day, so I brought you this."

Jessie saw he was carrying a tray containing several covered dishes, and realized she was starving. Now that Time-Out was hungry, she, too, was ravenous.

"Grab that stool over there," Jessie said, pointing across the barn, "so you can sit down, too."

Mr. Robeson dragged up a stool and stationed it alongside his daughter. "You aren't cold, are you?" he asked dotingly. "I also brought this." He offered her his old pea jacket. "I couldn't find any of your things," he explained.

Jessie was touched by her father's gesture and she smiled at him affectionately when he reached over and draped it across her shoulders. Then she attacked her food.

"Hey, this is good," she said between huge mouthfuls of potato salad. "And I think I recognize this . . ."—she took a taste of the egg noodle casserole that contained little bits of onion and lamb.

"Oh, yes." Her father suddenly burst out laughing.

"Leftovers from Grandma's roast leg of lamb with garlic again, I see," Jessie defined the concoction.

"It seems like we've been eating it every night for days," her father said. "At least since you've been away." Smiling, he added, "And to think I used to like it."

Jessie was suddenly serious. "Did she stay at the house when I was away?" she wanted to know.

"Yes," her father told her. "And that's something we're going to have to discuss."

Jessie finished eating and turned to look over

her shoulder and into the stall to make sure Time-Out was still okay. As a matter of fact, her horse had followed her example, and was now eating wholeheartedly.

"I know there's a lot we have to talk about, Dad." Jessie turned back to her father, wishing things could just automatically get better.

"Now isn't the right time," her father said, pulling his stool a little closer to her. "But I do want to tell you I've been thinking a lot about you over the past few days, and I want you to know I'm sorry if I've been too hard on you."

"I know ..." Jessie tried to express her feelings.

"But we're not going to go into all this now," her father insisted. "I only want to make one announcement, which I hope will be agreeable to you."

Jessie looked up at him with renewed interest.

"Of course, I had to call on your grandmother during your absence, since I'm back to work full-time now. The first day you were gone I realized how selfish I've been, Jessie, to think you could take care of all the chores alone. But there was the problem of finding a good housekeeper...."

Jessie nodded, riveted by what her father was saying.

"Anyway, after Grandma came for a couple of days, and after we all raved about her lamb and agreed we could put up with her cooking—if she would change the menu once in a while—she decided to move in with us and become Mother Hen again."

"Really?" Jessie was truly astonished.

"Well, the more we talked about it, the more we realized it was best for everyone. Grandma's been downright bored this past year, with nothing to do but play bridge and go to movies, and physically she's probably almost as strong as I am. She insists she wants to take over all the housework, cooking, shopping—everything. Sarah and Nick agree—if you'll cook once in a while so we can get a relief from that lamb!"

"Oh, Dad," Jessie responded. Why hadn't they thought of it before? It was the perfect solution.

"We all love Grandma, and now we'll be kind of an extended family," her dad concluded proudly. "What do you think?"

"I think it's brilliant," Jessie exclaimed, and threw her arms around his neck. It seemed as if she had never felt so relieved as she did now that she was about to reclaim her father.

"It's a beginning," he assured her. "And there are going to be a lot more changes around our house, too." He suddenly seemed very serious. "While you were gone, I realized that if I ever lost you, I would be losing the most precious thing in the world to me." He dropped his head to hide a sniffle.

The happy reunion between father and daughter was interrupted a few moments later by a full-fledged neigh from Time-Out.

"Oh, Silly." Jessie jumped up. "Don't think we've forgotten about you." She reached up and grabbed a dandy brush and began on Time-Out's neck and withers. "I'll be gentle," she told her. "You're just barely getting well."

"Any chance I could learn to do that?" her father asked, poking his head inside the stall.

Jessie looked up at him.

"Well." He beamed. "If I'm going to come and watch you two perform at Winsdor, I'd better know how to groom."

"Windsor!" Jessie exclaimed. "I can go to Windsor?"

Mr. Robeson nodded, and then turned to say hello to Anne, who had just entered the barn. Jessie heard him whisper a quick thanks under his breath, and she knew then that Anne must have been instrumental in helping him work things out.

"Thank God." Anne sighed when she saw Jessie brushing Time-Out. "It's all over. Now that she's over her crisis, it won't take her long to bounce back. You really can go home, you know, Jessie. We'll look after her."

"Oh, no," Jessie insisted. "I'd like to spend the night, if I could. I want to check her every so often, just to make sure she's absolutely well. If that's all right with you, Dad?"

"Sure," said Mr. Robeson. "Only try to get some sleep in between."

"If she keeps improving, you can give her a nice bran mash late this evening," Anne stated. "No carrots, though. We'll want to wait till she has some roughage back in her system."

Jessie nodded, and turned back to Time-Out.

They both had a long night ahead of them. Jessie set the alarm and got up every three hours to return to the barn and make sure the miracle had really happened. Time-Out was fully recov-

ered. It was on the last visit, early the next morning, after Jessie had presented her now-hungry
horse with a second delicious hot bran mash—
with carrots and extra molasses—that she heard
the sound of approaching footsteps.

"Hello, there." It was her father. "I thought you
might be finishing up by now." He peered over to
look at Time-Out. "How is she?"

"She's almost her old self," Jessie informed him.

"I stopped by because I thought I might give
you a lift home."

"You bet." She smiled and patted Time-Out.
"You'll be okay now, girl. As for me," she declared resolutely, "I'm ready to go home."

Chapter 12

"I really love your haircut, Jessie," Dara exclaimed.

"It's adorable!" Kate agreed. "You look so much older! Makes me wonder if I should get mine trimmed, too."

"Definitely not," Dara declared. "Your hair's got a little wave, and you look so great with it braided." She reached out and ran her hand through Kate's light blond, silky mane. "On the other hand," continued the expert, "Jessie can wear hers shorter because she's got that marvelous long neck. It makes her look so ... so really English, you know," Dara concluded.

"Good grief!" Kate howled and rolled her eyes. Dara was famous for her farfetched analyses of everything from haircuts to horse races.

Jessie looked up at the thin layer of gauzy clouds that raced across the turquoise sky. It was another Saturday morning at Windcroft, and for Jessie, life was finally getting somewhat back to normal. As they stood together near the practice ring waiting for their weekly instruction from Anne, the girls thought about only one thing: the up-coming competition at Windsor.

"The hairdresser assumed I was nuts when I insisted she cut it, after seeing it with my hard hat on," Jessie told them. "She finally got the idea I needed a haircut that went with the hard hat, so she agreed to do it." Jessie touched the back of her blunt-cut, collar-length hair and added, "Ac-tually, it's a little short now. But in another month, it'll be perfect."

"And I want you to look your very best, too," Jessie addressed Time-Out, who was tied up to the hitching post and was about to receive a thorough Saturday morning grooming. After being so sick, she really needed it.

"How're you feeling now, girl?" Kate inquired.

"Oh, she's as good as new," Jessie answered happily.

"Boy, you really gave us a scare," Dara gently scolded the horse, but at the same time patted her neck. "Don't you ever go and get sick on us again," she demanded. "Next time don't be such a glutton. Leave the moldy hay alone. And you," she said, addressing Jessie, "don't you ever disap-pear again, either."

"Get off it, Dara." Kate laughed. "You sound like someone's mother."

"Well," Dara whined, "I think I have a right to know where one of my best friends is spending the night. Especially if it's next door to her new boyfriend."

"Dara!" Jessie squealed. "For your information, I didn't go to Ogden to see Ed. I went to visit Lynne."

"Sure, sure, we know all about it," Dara kidded.

"Not to change the subject," Jessie went on as she reached for a dandy brush and began brushing Time-Out's hocks and buttocks, "but I haven't heard you mention Doug lately. Or for that matter . . ."—she turned to Kate, who was leaning up against the rail—"How's Pete?"

Kate informed her that Pete was fine, but Dara, the jokester, went on, "We've got our men all trained by now. When we're busy getting ready for a show, they don't come around and don't expect much attention. Except when we ring."

"Look who she's calling 'men,'" Jessie said and laughed. She finished with the dandy brush and reached for the softer body brush for Time-Out's neck and withers. The horse's sleek coat had already begun to gleam, and won the admiring glances of her friends.

Kate had climbed up to sit on the top rail of the fence, and she was now straining her neck to take in the full panoramic view of the farm and the trails beyond it. There was a faint tinge of burning leaves in the cool fall air, accompanied by the still-flamboyant visual backdrop of colorful foliage.

"I think fall's my favorite time of year," Kate concluded. She pulled up the collar of her navy blue wool jacket so it almost covered her ears.

"Yeah, if it weren't followed by winter," Dara agreed. She jumped up to sit beside Kate, and they looked as if they were part of an audience, viewing Jessie as she groomed her horse.

Done with the brushing and a thorough strapping with a wisp, Jessie wiped Time-Out's eyes and nose with a damp towel, and then grabbed the hoof pick to clean her hooves. Afterward she painted her hooves with Fiebing's Hoofoil. Time-Out was in seventh heaven, and hadn't complained once during the entire process.

"Oh, Jess, she looks just great," Kate commented. "We're so glad your dad is letting you go to Windsor, aren't we, Dara?"

"Yup," Dara confirmed. "It would have been a disaster for the Three Musketeers to be split up."

Jessie smiled as she carefully separated each hair of Time-Out's tail with her fingers. Like Time-Out, she, too, was feeling content and happy. It was so good to be back with her friends, and to have matters settled at home. Grandma had moved right in, and everything was working out just fine. As a matter of fact, all of the Robesons had agreed they were even becoming downright fond of lamb with garlic.

It seemed like it had been an eternity since Jessie had spent time just hanging out, talking with Kate and Dara. Now she was going to be included in all of the planning for Windsor, and her heart leapt at the thought of it.

"As much as I've enjoyed chatting with you ladies, I see that my trainer is ready," Kate said haughtily as she jumped down lightly to her feet. "Cheerio!" She waved and walked in the direction of her mother, who had motioned her to get going.

Anne had been busy setting up a line of fences, including both in-and-outs and bounces. After Kate and Spy circled the ring a few times to make sure Spy was properly warmed up, Kate sat quietly with her weight just behind the center of gravity.

When they took the first jump, she folded neatly over Spy's neck to avoid throwing him out of balance, and gently released the reins while still maintaining contact with his mouth. He sailed smoothly over the fence, and horse and rider sustained seemingly perfect harmony.

"Class act!" Dara and Jessie shouted from where they watched on the sidelines. The sight of Kate, with her good form, dressed as she was in jeans and chaps and a bright yellow sweatshirt, was like a splash of sunshine against the brown earth, and together, she and Spy made gold.

Kate and Spy repeated the line after Anne gave them a few helpful suggestions.

"You and Spy look absolutely wonderful," Anne declared proudly. All three girls were impressed, since they knew that Anne didn't hand out compliments loosely.

"Spy is finally relaxing over his fences, and he's starting to fold his legs and use his shoulders and back well."

"I'll say," Kate agreed. "His days of charging fences are long gone."

"Boy," Jessie exclaimed, totally impressed by the performance. "All of your hard work certainly is paying off. Keep it up and there'll be no doubt about your going Preliminary."

"Yes," Anne agreed immediately. "Spy looks so good today I think you are capable of advancing to Preliminary now, but my advice is to wait for spring and go Preliminary then, with the additional goal of doing one or maybe two three-day events in the fall."

Kate thought for a moment, and then agreed. "I

think that's what I want to do. By spring there won't be any doubt." She turned to address her horse. "Spy and I will have our act together."

"What about you, Dara?" Jessie asked.

"We already decided last weekend to wait, too. Didn't we, Anne?" Dara consulted her trainer.

"Yes. Arpeggio is close, but I think spring is a better time for her, too. If you wait until spring, there's a good chance of finishing in the ribbons, and that's always good for our big egos, you know."

Everyone laughed at Anne's frankness, and again when Kate said under her breath, "We all know Dara doesn't need any help with her ego. Especially when Doug is around."

"Kate!" Dara screamed. As brazen as Dara could sometimes be, even she was embarrassed to discuss boys in front of Kate's mother.

Jessie and Kate exchanged a private glance at the mention of Doug. Both knew that since Dara had developed a more communicative situation at home, she was no longer expected to be best at *everything* she did. Now she had an opportunity to be human, and since she and Doug seemed to trust each other and were really close friends, they had begun to spend a little more time together. The only consequence was the constant ribbing she got from her friends.

"I don't know anyone who likes to ride around in a car and listen to country music like you do, Dara. And eat ice cream. You must be the cheapest date around," Kate kidded her.

"Yeah," Jessie agreed. "When I start going out, my dates are going to take me to the ballet or the theater, and of course we'll probably attend the Derby and have a box seat at the finish line. I'll be on TV, pictured in my stylish gown and chapot."

"Fat chance!" Dara had laughed. "You've only been out on one date in your life, and that was to the movies."

"Don't remind her," Kate said firmly, putting an end to their frolic.

Boys were okay, Jessie thought now, but riding was something else. She watched Dara go through relaxed, supple exercises in the practice ring, and thought about how the year had progressed, and about how she could live without a boyfriend, but never without Time-Out. Happily, on this gorgeous Saturday in October, she was lucky enough to have both.

"I'll work with you this afternoon," Anne said to Jessie after Dara was finished and had cooled down Arpeggio. "Willy the blacksmith is here and I need to speak with him for a while."

"Does that mean what I think it does?" Dara asked delightedly. It looked to her as if they might have time to make a fast run to Lickety-Split. After all, now that Jessie was back and Time-Out was well, it was time to celebrate.

Kate and Jessie didn't take long to agree, and they all piled into Dara's car and headed toward town.

"Oink-Oink," all three girls said in unison when they entered the colorful ice-cream parlor, and then they covered their faces with their hands, dying of embarrassment.

Everyone knew that at Lickety-Split if a group of customers walked in and said "Oink-Oink" to-

gether, they would get a dish of ice cream that
had ten scoops of different flavors—plus all the
toppings—for just four dollars. It came in a giant
boat-shaped bowl, and all of the little piggies
were given spoons so they could eat it together.

Up until now, none of them believed they would
ever have the nerve to order it. It was so stupid.
But on the drive in, after several miles of shout-
ing and screaming, Dara had convinced Kate and
Jessie that upon the occasion of Jessie's home-
coming, they should go ahead and make fools of
themselves.

A few moments later they were faced with a
bright, gooey work of art, an ice-cream lover's
dream, a caloric creation that looked as if it would
take hours, days, to devour.

"Good-bye, lunch and dinner," Dara said happily, and dug her spoon into the chocolate.

"Good-bye, waistline," chimed in Jessie, and
began carving out the pistachio side of the
mountain.

"Hello, ecstasy," Kate concluded their little re-
quiem by plowing into the heavenly marshmallow
that was nearest her.

For several minutes the friends ate in silence,
drowning in the rich concoction before them and
sharing in the unspoken pleasure of being together again at Lickety-Split.

"So." Kate traded her spoon for a cup of water,
unable to stop talking for long. "We've got a plan.
We'll all go to Windsor next month, and then
we'll go back next spring, when Dara and I enter
Preliminary."

"Makes good horse sense to me," Dara said,

and they all approved the plan. Until Kate remembered they were forgetting something.

"Remember, Jess, you can't cop out on Time-Out. You are going to go Training, aren't you?"

Jessie paused for a suspenseful moment, and then announced, "I've talked with Anne, and we've decided that in four weeks, Jessica and Time-Out Robeson will enter Windsor at Training level."

"Hurray," Dara responded, momentarily diverted from her ice cream. She studied Jessie's face briefly and then added, "You know, Jess, a lot has happened to you this fall. Ever since that show in Ogden."

"Sure has," Kate agreed.

"Seems like a miracle or something," Jessie said. "Ever since I've been back, I feel like I can't scare up a single problem. My grandmother will barely let me do anything at home, and is doting on my father. His back is just about well now, and he's cracking jokes all the time! Grandma insists that the whole family go to Windsor to see me perform, and Sarah's so excited about it, she's told the entire school." Jessie radiated a new exuberance. "Why, I even got a B on an advanced algebra test last week. Now, that is a miracle."

"We're so happy for you," Kate said. "I told you everything was going to turn out okay," she said in an aside to Dara. Then again to Jessie: "We'd like to get to know your friend Lynne. She sounds neat."

"So does your boyfriend," Dara added.

"Maybe we can all go up there," Jessie suggested. "But you'll see them again soon at Windsor. Lynne's going for sure, and I'm pretty sure Ed will be there."

"Oh, goodie," Dara said. "That means we can put him through inspection; see if he meets with our approval."

"You do and I'll sic Doug on you." Jessie laughed. "Anyway," she added shyly, "you'll get to know him when he comes down for the Harvest Dance."

"Well, well, well," Dara chimed. "You've been holding out on us! Jessie has a date for the Harvest Dance before Pete or Doug have even so much as thought about it."

"Since he asked me about Thanksgiving, I mentioned it, and ..." Jessie *was* embarrassed. The two-hour phone conversation she had had with Ed after he called to find out about Time-Out had resulted in his insisting they make a real date—even if he had to use visiting his cousin Bruce, who lived nearby in Connecticut, as an excuse to come see her. What could be more appropriate than the Harvest Dance?

Not only my first real date, Jessie thought, smiling, but also my first formal dance.

"How do you feel?" Dara suddenly asked. The ice-cream boat was almost empty.

"Stuffed!" pronounced Jessie. She threw down her spoon.

"Not so good," Kate said after realizing just how much she had eaten.

"I think we should be congratulated," Dara decided. "We started it and we finished it. Doesn't matter if we'll all have stomachaches for a few hours." She squeezed out of the booth and got to her feet.

"Speaking of finishing things ..."—Jessie got up, too—"I've got to get back and take my lesson."

"Well, my fellow riders," Kate predicted after the three girls left the shop and were strolling down the street toward the car, "we're headed for something that's gonna be a lot harder than getting dates or finishing a gallon of ice cream. We'd better start hoping for some good luck and a few more miracles at Windsor."

"Ah, I don't know," Jessie answered. "Miracles are one thing. They just sorta happen. But Windsor is something else. You gotta do that yourself. I've already had a talk with Time-Out. Her getting well was our miracle, and we're both thankful for it, but now we're gonna work superhard for the next month to get the dressage test down pat."

Jessie paused, and in the next decisive moment she stopped and turned to her friends. "So shine up the window and make room in the showcase, Kate, 'cause when the Windcroft riders—and their talented horses—enter the ring, the whole world had better be ready. We're going to bring home the ribbons!"

GLOSSARY

BIT: A metal or rubber bar that is fit into the horse's mouth to help control the horse's direction and speed; part of the bridle.

BLAZE: A striking white marking of medium width that runs down the middle of a horse's face.

BREECHES: Riding pants, usually of a tight stretch material, that fit closely over the calves and are worn inside riding boots.

BROODMARE: Female horse used specifically for breeding.

BRIDLE: Headgear consisting of head and throat straps, bit, and reins. Used for controlling a horse.

CANTER: A rolling three-beat gait, faster than a trot.

CAVALLETT: A series of long poles of adjustable height, supported by crossbars; used in teaching both horses and riders to jump.

CONFORMATION: A horse's proportionate shape or contour.

CRIB: A type of bin used to hold food for stable animals; "cribbing" is also a bad habit of horses who bite the edges of doors, feed bins, etc. while sucking in air.

CROSS-COUNTRY: A timed event that takes place on open land. These courses include riding across fields, through woods, and along trails and require jumping over natural and man-made barriers such as ditches, logs, and hedges.

CROSS-TIES: A pair of leads, one attached to the right side of the halter and one to the left, used for holding the horse in place while grooming.

CURRY: To rub and clean a horse with a *curry comb*, which is a round rubber comb that loosens mud, dried sweat, and hair.

DIAGONAL: In riding, refers to the rider's position at the posting trot as the horse moves diagonal pairs of legs. On a circle, the rider would be rising in the saddle as the horse's outside shoulder moves forward (and the inside shoulder moves back). This keeps the rider from interfering with the horse's balance and freedom of movement.

DRESSAGE: Training a horse to perform with increased balance, suppleness and obedience, and to perfect its paces. A dressage test involves a traditional system of complex maneuvers performed in an arena in front of one or more judges. The test is scored on each movement and on the overall impression that horse and rider make.

EVENT: Also known as *Horse Trial.* A competitive series of exercises which test a horse's strength, obedience and intelligence. Also used as a verb:

"Now she has a horse of her own to ride and *event.*"

EVENTING: Also known as *combined training* and *three-day eventing.* A series of tests combining dressage, jumping and cross-country competitions.

FARRIER: A person who shoes horses; blacksmith.

FETLOCK: The horse's ankle; a projection bearing a tuft of hair on the back of a horse's leg, above the hoof and the pastern.

FILLY: A female horse less than four years of age.

FLANK: On a horse, the fleshy part of the side between the ribs and the hip.

FOAL: A horse under one year of age. Foals are usually weaned at six months and are then called weanlings. Also, to give birth to a horse.

FOALING BOX: A structure used as a maternity ward for expectant mares, usually designed with a gap in the wall so that labor and birth may be observed secretly.

GAITS: General term for all the foot movements of a horse: walk, trot, canter, or gallop.

GALLOP: The horse's fastest gait, although there are gradations; an open gallop is faster than a hard gallop.

GELDING: A male horse that has been castrated for the purpose of improving the animal's temper and health.

GIRTH: A sturdy strap and buckle for securing the saddle.

GROOM: To clean and care for an animal. Also the person who performs these tasks.

HALT: In dressage, bringing the horse to an absolute stop with all four feet square and straight.

HALF-HALT: A subtle signal that encourages the horse to gather himself, improving his balance and preparing him for a change of pace or direction.

HALTER: A loose-fitting headgear with a noseband, and head and throat straps to which a lead line may be attached.

HANDS: A unit used to measure a horse's height, each hand equaling 4 inches. A horse is measured from the ground to his withers. Ponies stand up to 14 hands 2 inches (14½ hands) high; larger horses are everything above. A 15-hand horse stands 5 feet high at his withers.

HAY RACK: A rack for holding hay for feeding horses.

HOOFPICK: A piece of grooming equipment used to gently clean dirt and stones from between hoof and horseshoe.

IMPULSION: The horse shows willingness to move freely, particularly through the powerful driving action of its hindquarters.

IN AND OUT: Two fences positioned close to each other and related in distance, so that the horse must jump "in" over the first fence and "out" over second.

JODHPURS: Riding pants cut full through the hips and fitted closely from knee to ankle.

JUMPING: In eventing, also known as *stadium jumping*.

Horse and rider must take and clear ten to twelve fences in a ring. Penalty points are added for refusals, falls, and knockdowns.

LATERAL MOVEMENT: When a horse moves sideways and forward at the same time.

LEAD: The piece of rope or leather used to lead a horse.

LIPPIZANER: A compact, handsome horse, usually gray, originally bred at the Lipizza Stud near Trieste; famous for their use in dressage exhibitions at the Spanish Riding School in Vienna.

MUCKING OUT: To clear manure and soiled bedding from a horse stall.

OXER: A jump or obstacle that requires the horse to jump width as well as height.

PADDOCK: An enclosed outdoor area where horses are turned out and exercised.

PACE: The speed at which a horse travels, or, in harness racing, a two-beat gait in which the legs on the same side of the horse move in unison.

PALOMINO: Technically a color rather than a breed; a type of horse developed mainly in the Southwestern United States. These animals have golden coats and flaxen or white manes and tails.

POST: Rising up and down out of the saddle in rhythm with the horse's trot.

SADDLE FLAPS: Side pieces on an English saddle. They hide the straps needed to keep the saddle in place.

SERPENTINE: In dressage, a series of equal curves from one side of the ring's center line to the other. The horse changes the direction of his turn each time he passes over the centerline.

SHOULDER: A lateral movement in which the horse moves sideways and forward at the same time, bending his body around the rider's leg.

STANDARD: An upright post used to support the rail of a hurdle.

STIRRUP-LEATHERS: The strap used to suspend a stirrup from a saddle.

TACK: The gear used to outfit a horse for riding, such as saddle, halter, and bridle.

TROT: A two-beat gait faster than a walk, in which the horse's legs move in diagonal pairs (left forward, right rear).

WITHERS: The ridge between a horse's shoulder bones. The highest point above the shoulders where the neck joins the back.

Here's a look at what's ahead in THE MAIN EVENT, the sixth book in Fawcett's "Blue Ribbon" series for GIRLS ONLY.

Kate finished checking Spy's coat for dirt and reached for his blanket. Her moods had been hurtling on a roller coaster for more than a day now. She was thrilled at Spy's performance in the dressage—theirs had been the top score by far—and yet her anxiety over her feelings for Pete and his moving made her feel miserable. "I don't know which end is up," she muttered as she plopped down onto a stool.

"That makes two of us." Pete reached down to lift her to her feet, holding her hands longer than was really necessary. For a long, wonderful moment they gazed at each other, heedless of Northern Spy's whinny. How come you're not paying attention to me? he seemed to be demanding.

But when Pete drew Kate into his arms, neither of them noticed Spy. They kissed, and as the kiss deepened, their arms closed tightly around each other. Kate closed her eyes, reveling in the wonderful sensation of floating while standing still. Of all the marvelous things she associated with Pete, this was what she would miss the most.

The insistent neigh from Spy's stall broke their embrace, but Kate felt so warm and happy that she didn't mind. "Okay, Spy, you old prima donna. You've got my complete attention." She slipped out of Pete's arms and circled the horse, latching together the various hooks on his complicated blanket. "Feel better now?" she asked him, tousling his forelock.

"We probably upset him," Pete suggested. "He's probably never seen anybody kissing before."

Kate brushed down her old jeans, checking for bits of straw that could more profitably be left in the stall than on her bedroom floor. "He's just mad because we're not kissing him," she declared.

So far they had successfully avoided the subject neither of them wanted to discuss. But for both of them, it loomed as the most ominous thought in their minds. Finally Kate broke into it, in her straightforward way. "Have you heard from your folks?" she asked.

He gazed down at the barn floor. "Mom called late this afternoon. She said they've found a couple of places they like a lot. They want me to come up next weekend and check them out."

"You mean you make the final decision about where you're going to live?" How grisly, Kate thought. Like choosing the method of execution in your own death.

Pete nodded. "They're trying so hard to be fair to me—"

"But being fair to you would mean staying here," Kate finished. They gripped each other's hands tightly for a moment. Then, before she could speak, Pete whirled around and slammed his fist into the side of the barn.

"This is crazy!" he cried. "My whole life's being ripped up in little pieces right in front of me!"

"Pete, for heaven's sake, you'll frighten the horses—"

Pete stopped himself and turned to her. His breath was coming in gasps. "I *hate* this!" he blurted out finally. "I hate looking at the calendar and knowing that every day that goes by means one less day in Smithfield. I hate your competitions, because they mean you can't spend time with me. I hate everything!"

Kate started to walk toward him, to reach out her arms to him. Pete looked as though he were going to burst apart. He stormed up and down in front of her.

"I've got to find a way to make things work!" Suddenly, to her astonishment, he wheeled and darted away, leaving her in the shadows of the barn. In a moment, she heard the cough of his car engine, then the crunch of tires on gravel as he sped off.

The
BLUE RIBBON
Series

*Discover the exciting world
of thoroughbred horse competition*